HOT AS HADES

ALISHA RAI

ALISHA RAI

DEAR READER:

Thank you so much for reading this rerelease of Hot as Hades. This novella was originally published in 2010, and for this new edition, I've taken the liberty of making some edits, though the plot of the story remains roughly the same. Below is my original author's note.

Usually when people ask me where I get my ideas, I have no response for them that won't somehow sound emo. Not this time. I've always had a passionate interest in mythology, and it was recently rekindled when I toured the British Museum. As I stood in front of a relief of Hades abducting Persephone, I started to daydream about the infamous couple. After I left the museum, the daydreaming wouldn't stop. Yet my romance-author brain had issues with Hades and his hero viability. Abduction? Trickery to force the girl to stay? Plus, it had always skeeved me out that Persephone was technically Hades's niece on both sides, since she was the daughter of his sister and his brother. No, that wouldn't do.

So I changed all of those things, and some other stuff too.

Dear Reader:

If you're familiar with the myth, I'm sure you noticed, and I hope you appreciated and will forgive my reworking of the tale. If you aren't, well, just know that I indulged in some artistic meddling.

Either way, I hope you enjoyed my adaptation.

1

———

Hades, a.k.a. The Unseen One, a.k.a. The Awe-Inspiring Lord of the Underworld, was accustomed to souls dropping into his kingdom. The fortunate and unfortunate, his subjects and servants, they came with nothing.

However, that didn't mean they were naked. Or flesh-and-blood. Or dropped literally into his lap.

"Well hello," he said to the wet, naked, shaking, warm, soft—and wait, did he mention naked?— woman sprawled over him, straddling him where he sat on his mighty throne. "Can I help you?"

Rapid panting was her only response. Her breath skimmed over his neck where her face was buried. All he could see was hair, wild waves of damp black silk which covered her back.

He could feel quite a bit, though his vision was obscured by her springy mane. Her arse was round and full, nestled upon his thighs. Hard nipples drilled into his bare chest where her breasts flattened against him. Her heart pounded in triple time.

Clap her in chains and demand an accounting of her presence.

Yes, that's what he should do, obviously. He wasn't a fool. He had more enemies than he did friends, and he wasn't about to assume anything out of the ordinary in his realm was benign.

Instead he inhaled, pulling her scent into his lungs. It was a foreign smell. Sweet, and...floral?

She raised her head and straightened away from him with some effort, shaking her hair back from her face. He could at least see her face now, which was nice. Alas, her breasts were no longer squished against him. That was not nice.

Her eyes were stunning chips of emerald ice, perfect except for the dazed confusion in them. No fault could be found with the rest of her— smooth bronze skin, full ruby red lips and a face that was so perfectly carved, it could have been mounted on any temple wall. His sharp gaze catalogued her pretty face quickly and followed the glistening rivulets of water down her body to what he could see of her flesh playing peekaboo with that glorious hair. Her breasts were firm and large, the nipples brown and tightening from the cool of the room. The rest of her was similarly lush— round, soft thighs, the heat of which he could feel through his leather pants, that healthy handful of a derriere nestled against his crotch, wide hips and a tangle of black curls over her mound that looked as touchable as the strands on her head.

Her heart continued to beat fast, he noted, as he tried to drag his gaze back up to her face. No, wait. She wasn't pressed against him any more. That was *his* heart.

"Hello." He purred the word this time. His hands automatically clamped over her giving, wondrous hips when she shifted.

You're not going anywhere.

"Where...? Who...?" A frown pleated her smooth forehead and she shifted, raising a hand to her temple, as if she had a ferocious headache.

The light from the gas lamp closest to him fell on her upraised arm. The flame danced along her skin, her sudden motion bringing out a heretofore unnoticed pearlescent glow. The subtle inhuman coloring made his breath catch. Not in lust.

In fury. "Goddess," he spat out. His hands tightened. Oh no, she definitely wasn't going anywhere now.

He didn't know if it was the venom in his tone or his harder grip that jolted her. Her lashes fluttered as she blinked and shook her head once. Rapid-fire emotions flickered over that heart-shaped face— confusion gave way to fear which gave way to horror when she glanced down and took in her lack of clothes. With a small, feminine shriek, she pushed her hands against his chest and tried to launch herself out of his grasp. It was laughably easy to subdue her by wrapping his arms around her and pinning her hands between them.

Those unearthly eyes narrowed. "Release me, you sick bastard."

He considered that laughable edict for all of, oh, point three seconds. Release a goddess, probably here to murder him, or worse, seduce him? "No thanks."

"That's an order, not a request."

"I never did take orders well." Along with his inability to share his toys, it was one of his many vices.

Her little stubborn chin lifted in an annoyingly regal manner, as if she was the one in the throne and not naked and subdued in his arms. "Release me, or suffer."

"Suffer what?"

"Suffer...my wrath."

"Aren't you cute."

Those pretty lips thinned. "Even if you aren't scared of me, you should be terrified of my family."

He raised an eyebrow, equally amazed and impressed that she dared to threaten him. "*I'll* be terrified of your family, eh?"

"Yes."

"Do you have any idea who I am?"

"Nope. Don't know, don't care, and I particularly don't like that you stole me out of my bath to fondle me and ask me stupidly irrelevant questions. I promise you, sir, my family will rip you limb from limb for abducting me."

Seriously? She actually thought he would be fooled by her going on the offense? He used his grip to pull her closer, savoring her gasp of outrage and that odd, unidentifiable scent that teased his nostrils. "I ripped you from nowhere. I was minding my business when you tumbled straight into my lap."

She may not care who he was, but he cared who she was. Some minor deity? Granted, he never left the Underworld anymore, but he knew most everyone at Olympus by description, if not by sight. No one had ever described someone so...delicious.

"Lies. You're saying that I happened to step out of my river and, with no foul play, fell into..." She looked around and froze.

His decorating skills were amazing, in his opinion, but he was aware his home wasn't to everyone's taste.

"Are those...are those skulls mounted into the walls?"

He dipped his head. They were the finest skulls fear could buy, but he didn't like to brag.

"Your door handle is a femur."

"Belonged to a famous Hollywood executive," he said with pride. He didn't like to brag *much*. The powerful businessman had accomplished a stunning array of evil things in his life, and it had brought Hades much joy to install that handle, while the man's soul watched. Torture didn't always involve physical pain.

She didn't look impressed by his boast. Did he need to go into more gory detail? Because he *could*.

"Where the hell am I?"

What an actress. Since he was half-enjoying the novelty of this playacting, he replied. "Yes."

"What?"

"You're in Hell. The Underworld, love. To be more specific, you're currently in the throne room of the palace of the almighty and great ruler of said Underworld."

She swallowed, and didn't that just conjure up all sorts of dirty thoughts? "Which would make you...?"

He bowed his head in greeting. "Hades. I know, you're wildly pleased to make my acquaintance."

"Dark One."

He stiffened. The tremor of fear in her voice was evident. Though he knew this must be an act, a sharp pang hit him.

Why shouldn't she be afraid? She'd probably been told all her life what a mad, bad bastard of a god he was.

All those rumors really made him want to live up to that hype. She should be afraid. Everyone should.

"Send me back."

"Once again: I didn't bring you here." No doubt she'd hoped to slip in, accomplish whatever foul deed she was up to and slip away again, with him none the wiser. Like that was possible—if a soul passed gas down here, he heard about it. How she had managed to enter his palace at all was a mystery, one he'd be solving immediately. The only god or goddess who was powerful enough to conceivably break past his many safeguards into the Underworld was Zeus—and baby brother knew better than to interfere in Hades's job.

Long story short, beautiful or not, this little goddess should be perched on a cloud somewhere and not his lap. He gave her one last chance. "Let's start with your name, goddess."

Her mouth set in a mulish line. "Bite me."

Hades's blood fired at the flat refusal. "Would love to. First things first." Keeping her pinned with one hand, he grasped her chin with the other and stared into her eyes.

Reading a mortal's past was child's play—he looked at a soul, and the person's history was an open book, every thought, every screwup, every moment of rapture projected into his brain in Technicolor.

Deities were harder, but not impossible. He could get snatches of their life story here and there, particularly if they were lesser gods and goddesses.

Her power hit him harder than he'd hit that Hollywood executive, slamming him out of her brain and life.

This woman was no lesser goddess.

Facing a power that possibly rivaled even his awesome talents was a little like staring at the sun. It blinded him to everything else. With sheer force of will, he gritted his teeth and attempted to at least study the delicate core of strength for any familiar traces. Genetics were everything in their circle. If he knew her father or mother, he could potentially use that knowledge to fight her.

Unfortunately, this conglomeration of power was utterly foreign to him, which meant she hadn't been born of any deity he was familiar with, including his siblings. Not that he had really thought she was of his blood. When one overthrew one's parents, one got in the habit of keeping tabs on one's remaining family members and their offspring.

He had to close his eyes from the effort it took to dig out even that small scrap of information. When she commenced her feeble squirming, he opened them. His suspicions, already heightened, grew even more now that he was aware of the depth of her power. He wasn't holding her that tight. Why wasn't she fighting him?

Unless, of course, this show of weakness was all part of her plan. Her plot. Her plot to...well, do something. If that was the case, she'd underestimated him.

"Maybe you didn't hear me, Goddess. Name, purpose for being here. Or we do it the hard way." Because the easy way, plucking her memories out of her brain, wasn't an option any longer, but she didn't know that.

"Maybe you didn't hear me. Let. Me. Go." She punctuated each word with a jerk of her body.

Hard way, then. "And maybe I'll keep you right here, since you so conveniently threw yourself at me." Though he meant his words as a threat, he found the thought of keeping this stranger naked, bound and at his mercy particularly attractive. It had been too long since he'd had someone as lovely as her tempting him. Mortal souls threw themselves at him all the time, of course, but after centuries, that desperation and sick fascination had lost its appeal, if it had ever been there to begin with. He hadn't left his world to seek sexual partners, mortal or immortal, in a long time.

He waited for her to quit this act and break his hasty bond, but instead she looked down her nose at him and sniffed, the very picture of courage in the face of a fate worse than death. If he didn't know better, he might actually believe in her innocence.

"You have a lovely body."

She snorted. "I know."

His lips curved despite himself. "No modesty?"

"What good is modesty? Many men have found my body appealing."

Was that a hint of bitterness he heard? "Ah. Are you a disciple of Aphrodite, then?"

"I'm under no obligation to tell you anything. Release me and send me back to my river."

"Your river? Are you part nymph?" He could see her as a water nymph, those svelte, accommodating creatures, with their slick bodies and slicker...

Ah, he'd had some good times with nymphs in his youth.

"Are you deaf? I'm not telling you anything." She squirmed again, like that futile motion would accomplish anything.

"By all means, keep moving. I'm enjoying it."

She froze, her eyes shooting sparks at him. A curl shimmied with the force of her outrage. Her hair was starting to frizz, little hairs popping above her hairline. "How dare you...?"

"My house, my rules."

"Zeus—"

Just the sound of that name made him want to strip his clothes off and roll around naked in broken glass. There was no love lost between him and his siblings. Particularly since he knew any of them would cheerfully cut his throat if it gained them an ounce of power. "Zeus has no say here. This is my world, and you breached it. Surely you've heard of how I deal with trespassers. If I want to imprison you in Tartarus, no one would intervene. If I wanted to toss you to my demons, same. Is that what you want? Did you ignore an age-old treaty and come out for a jaunt just to play big bad hellhound and the scared little pussy?" Hell, that was a plausible and not an altogether unwelcome scenario. Morbid sexual fascination wasn't limited to desperate mortal souls, he supposed. Though if that was the case, it might be the first time he was tempted to satisfy the curiosity.

"Listen, you backwards behemoth. You may have the upper hand now, but you so much as think of harming me, I'll kill you."

He smirked. "Do it, then—" His words ended in a shout as sharp pain lanced through his arms, his chest, his legs, every part of him that touched her.

He shoved her off his lap in a move that was more violent than he intended. He had the presence of mind to materialize a plush pillow to cushion her ass before it could land on the marble floor of his throne room. She rose up on her hands and shoved her hair out of her face.

He examined his palms, but there were no puncture wounds.

He rose to his feet and gazed down at the goddess from his superior height. She was voluptuous, but small. He allowed himself to grow larger, adding a foot to his already formidable height. "What did you do just now?" he rasped.

"N-n-nothing."

Bullshit. It had felt like she'd sunk a thousand thorns into his flesh. "I'm going to put you in the deepest prison I can find. A dark pit where snakes will crawl over you for eternity and no one will hear you scream."

Fear flashed in her eyes and she sank back. He was happy she was finally cowering from him.

Are you?

Yes. He was thrilled. This was his thrilled face.

"Please, no."

He huffed out a breath. Smoke came out of his nostrils, a sign of the rage he'd learned to control in his adolescence. "You crash into my home, refuse to tell me even your name. Why shouldn't I imprison you?" Another tendril of smoke, and he grew another foot. "Are you here to steal a soul?" Some might say he was overly paranoid about any souls leaving his kingdom, but it was with good reason. Leaving the underworld caused shockwaves across all the realms.

"No! No, listen. I have no idea what I'm doing here either. My name's Persephone."

The name meant nothing to him. "Go on."

The beauty sighed. "Persephone, daughter of Demeter."

Shit. A shock of distaste and outrage ran through him. "Daughter of Demeter?" He wanted to hit something. He, who knew better than anyone that life was absolutely, motherfucking unfair, wanted to rail at the fates for this.

Not. Fucking. Fair.

2

Persephone stared up at the towering giant above her. He'd grown larger with his anger, a party trick she might be fascinated by if she wasn't so confused. His thighs looked like tree trunks under his black leather pants. The bulge at his crotch was prominent, despite the fact that he was looking at her with dismay instead of lust now. He would have been intimidating even if she wasn't sprawled naked at his feet. Even if she wasn't struggling with a never-before-experienced combination of fear and alarm and...was that arousal?

She shivered and she couldn't even blame that involuntary reflex on a draft. Though she was naked and the huge room appeared cold with its black granite walls and black marble floor, it was actually surprisingly warm. There was no sunlight, but flickering torches gave off light. Larger lamps stood near the huge red and black throne she had landed in, gilding every inch of Hades.

And there were a lot of inches. Despite her isolation from the rest of Olympus, she'd heard rumblings about Hades, as she had about Zeus and Poseidon, the three big honchos. Her adoptive mother, Demeter, was closemouthed about other deities, but Persephone had friends amongst the water nymphs. The only thing the nymphos—their term, not hers—liked as much as sex was gossip. So of course she'd heard whispers about the scary, merciless, pitiless, torture-and-pain-happy Lord of the Underworld.

Some of the older nymphs had also whispered that he was really fucking sexy too, but Persephone had discounted those as romanticized fantasies.

Not now she didn't. The male was devastatingly attractive, like no one she'd ever seen, either in her humble youth with mortals, her brief time amongst the foppish court at Olympus, or her return to Earth to live with Demeter. Blue-black hair was cropped close to his skull, and his face was hard and defined, with a square jaw and high cheekbones. Gold glinted in the simple armbands around his massive biceps. He was shirtless, which allowed her to see his ripped chest and abdomen. A tattoo highlighted those muscles, an intricate design of a red and black serpent. The snake's tongue flicked his nipple, its sinuous body draped across his chest, presumably wound around his back, and then came back around his hip to disappear into his pants.

She tried not to think of where the tail of that snake ended.

Hades's eyes were his most fascinating feature, black and endless, and glowing from within with a red fire.

Now they were filled with cold fury. And why not? Her mother's name alone was generally enough to rile and inspire the wrath of any god, which was why Persephone had hoped to keep mum about her mum and get herself out of here before Hades discovered her identity. How Demeter managed to piss off every deity she came into contact with,

Hot as Hades 13

save Persephone, she would never know. *Brazen it out, girl.* "I take it you have some sort of beef with Demeter?"

"Your mommy always was a self-righteous, selfish little bitch, chick."

Caution told her to curb her tongue, but she couldn't stop the small burst of anger. Whatever her faults, Demeter had done her best to be a mentor and protector to a lost, clueless goddess. "Watch how you speak of my mother, dark one."

"I'll call my *sister* whatever names I like, Sephie."

"The name is Persephone and...what? Wait. Sister?"

He sneered. "Whiny, bitchy Demeter is my little sister. Surely you knew that, if you're her daughter."

"I...I'm sorry. I've never really paid attention to all the relationships." And interrelationships. After millennia, blood relations seemed to matter less and less, she supposed. The gods married and mated with little concern for something that troubled mortals to no end.

He was shaking his head, disgust curling his lips as he repeatedly wiped his hand—the hand he'd held her with—on the front of his thighs. "I can't believe I... Why the hell didn't you say something sooner?" He swallowed. "Seriously, put some clothes on."

"I'd love to, but my luggage seems to have been lost." Dumbass, she added silently.

"Adorable. Conjure the clothes, wench."

A blush rose in her cheeks. Did he think she liked sitting here nude? "I can't."

"You can't now or you can't ever?"

"Can't...ever." Persephone raised her chin, unhappy in admitting to something that was probably possible for godlings. Maybe he would let this proof of her shameful lack of abilities pass without comment.

"Stop fooling around and get dressed."

No, he wouldn't let it pass. "I told you, I can't." Pretty and stupid, she tsked. They always went hand in hand, it seemed. Though Hades didn't seem quite as bad as Narcissus. That fool regularly had to be rescued from lakes when he tried to make out with his own reflection.

Hades studied her with his brow knit, though this time he kept his gaze on her face. "You're serious. You really can't." Within a blink she was clothed in a flowing red gown of velvet trimmed with black lace.

It was the most decadent thing she'd ever worn. Unable to help herself, she ran her hand along the drape of fabric over her leg.

His groan made her glance up, and she flushed again to see him watching her hand coast along her leg. Their eyes met, and the self-disgust in his was readily apparent. "You should have said something sooner, niece."

She blinked up at him. His *niece*, because she was Demeter's *daughter*. Well then. She glanced away, unclear on how to use this development to her advantage.

Something must have given her away; she'd always been a crappy liar. Suddenly he had shrunk to his earlier—still scary size—and was crouched next to her, his hand on her chin, giving her no choice but to turn her head to him. He stared deep into her eyes before a smile broke out on that stunning face. "Liar."

She played dumb. "Huh?"

"I should have known—after all, I'm never wrong," he arrogantly stated. "You aren't of my blood." He gave her chin a little shake, which made her instinctively snap at his fingers with her teeth. He only laughed. "You're no more Demeter's daughter than I am."

She pulled away from him, scooting out of his reach—it

Hot as Hades

annoyed her further that she wouldn't have been able to had he not allowed it. "You can't tell that by looking at me."

"Actually, I can. One of my dubious powers—to see what blood flows through others. Comes in handy when I have to deal with as many souls as I do. You aren't of my bloodline, which means you weren't born to any of my siblings. So tell me the truth now, Sephie...if that's even your real name."

"It is. I... Can you see who my parents really are?" she asked, distracted for a moment.

He cocked his head. "You're...foreign. Not quite like anyone I've looked into before."

"Oh." She didn't know if she absolutely believed him or not. Gods were notorious liars, after all.

"The truth. Now." His tone was hard and brooked no disobedience.

Sadly, as much as she wanted to tell him to go to hell, one thing was true. She was already there—and he owned it. "Demeter cared for me after I finally came to Olympus." Demeter had approached her at first because their powers were similar, and had ended up becoming a friend, mentor and a maternal figure, protecting her from the cattiness and advances of the other gods on Olympus. She'd also given Persephone whatever love and tenderness she was capable of. No, Demeter had her faults, no doubt, but Persephone would have probably withered away long ago without her.

"She's nothing more than a mentor, then," he purred. "Well now, bit. That's music to my ears." A finger stroked along her cheek, awakening all sorts of nerve endings.

What was wrong with her? Usually she was quite immune to the unearthly beauty of immortals. When she'd first come to Olympus, she'd realized quickly that she was the equivalent of the new girl at school, which meant that every god and goddess wanted to either fuck her or rip her hair out by the roots and set her on fire. Demeter, who had thankfully taken her under her wing, conferred with Zeus, and before Persephone could say "Apollo, you ignorant slut," she'd been spirited out of Olympus back to Earth.

End result: except for some fumbled flirting and sex with mortals, and again in the beginning of her foray into the world of the gods, it had been a long, dry, isolated spell for her. And it wasn't like any of those spoiled, pampered Olympians had even a hint of the raw sex appeal of Hades.

Hades, Lord of the Underworld, you fool. Slap a virtual chastity belt on, and pull yourself together.

Bad boys were bad for a reason, and she had zero experience in dealing with them. It wouldn't do to start with the ultimate bad boy. She shouldn't be here, didn't belong here. She belonged back home, in her safe and protected bubble, surrounded by meadows and rivers and babbling brooks. "Our lack of blood relation changes nothing."

He didn't appear to be listening, so transfixed was he with tracing his finger over the bodice of the dress, following the lace trim. It scratched her skin, making her want to rip the dress off and throw herself at him. She wanted to tell herself it was the fact that she'd been without for so long, but she'd never had such an instantaneous response to anyone, ever, god or mortal.

Fear trumped the arousal.

Since she couldn't fight with her fists, she would do what she'd always done and rely on her words. "Excuse me. I'm not about to get horizontal with the Lord of the Underworld. If you try something, know it would be against my will."

She tensed. The gods she'd met hadn't been well-versed in the concept of consent, so she half-expected him to bear her back onto the ground and ravish her, or maybe even manhandle her into a cell somewhere.

His anger and demands to know her identity seemed genuine. Since he thought she was the intruder, nobody would interfere with any punishment he extracted from her. She'd heard enough stories about Hades's almost obsessive territoriality about his world. No one who entered left it. Or at least, no one left it unscathed.

But he did none of those things. A chill descended over his face, turning those hot eyes to ice. His tone was similarly cold. "I don't rape."

She believed him again, oddly enough. "Then send me back to my home." Though pleading went against her nature, she swallowed her pride. "Please. I swear, I didn't bring myself here. I really did just step out of my bath and into your..." She gestured to encompass the throne room, avoiding looking at all the skulls.

He leaned back on his haunches and studied her closely. "You honestly don't know how you escaped my grip. Or how to conjure clothes."

Though he didn't seem to be waiting for a response, she shook her head.

"And you can't send yourself back?"

More pride swallowing. "If you can't tell yet, I don't have many powers. I wouldn't have the foggiest notion of how to transport myself anywhere in my own world, let alone across worlds."

He gave a short laugh, and she thought she heard him mutter to himself, "She has no idea."

"Excuse me?"

Hades raised his voice. "Very well."

She scrambled to her feet, and he rose as well, more slowly. "What?" Had she misheard? That had been too easy.

His eyes narrowed. "Did you think me so lacking in decency that I would imprison you when you didn't knowingly invade my domain? No, wait. Don't answer that. It's clear what you think. Go home, Persephone, daughter of Demeter. Make sure you tell your mama and the other ass-lickers up on that mountain how awful and evil Uncle Hades was, 'kay?"

Damn the pinch of guilt. She opened her mouth to recall her words. "I—"

He cut her off, raising his hand in a short, sharp gesture. Unable to help her body's response, she flinched.

"If I wanted to hit you, I would have already," he growled. "Now, begone, woman."

Sad, she thought, as she prepared herself for that dizzying rush of energy, that the last image she would retain of him was such a frightening one, with his face tightened in disgust and anger.

But her earthly meadow didn't suddenly rise up to embrace her, nor did she see the beautiful architecture and people of Olympus.

His anger dissipated into confusion. "Why are you still here?"

She shook her head, off balance from the slew of emotions running through her. "I don't know."

He raised his hand again, but she remained in front of him. "What the fuck?" He tipped his head back and roared, "Cerberus!"

"You rang, master?"

Hades moved aside, and Persephone gasped. Behind him stood a dog. A dog with three heads instead of one. This was the famed Cerberus, the most fearsome companion to Hades. He was huge, his body easily coming to her chest and covered in sleek midnight-black fur. Only the center head matched the body. The one on the right was a pure white, while the one on the left was tawny yellow. Their eyes were identical, fierce and black, and they glowed with the same red fire as Hades's gaze. Most pertinent to her state of mind, they all had really sharp, shiny teeth. *The better to eat me with.*

Hades pointed at her. "Why is she here?"

All three heads cocked. The middle head, whom she assumed was the mouthpiece of the group, spoke. "I am not sure, sire. I saw the ripple when this intruder breached our world. I assumed, since she entered your throne room, you summoned her."

"I bloody hell did not summon her. I didn't summon her, and now I can't send her back. Why the fuck is that?"

"I am unsure, sire. Everything is functioning fine in the rest of the realm. Souls are still coming in. Try again."

They both looked at her, and she prepared for the mind-jarring, nauseating rush of energy she'd experienced when she'd been sucked down here after stepping out of her bath.

Nope. Nada.

A deep growl of anger resonated from Hades's chest, turning gradually into a full-fledged roar, startling her. "Someone's blocking me. Who the fuck would dare to interfere with my world?"

Not her, she thought privately when he turned those endless eyes on her. Geez, when they called Hades territorial, they weren't kidding. He was incandescently angry at even the idea of someone interfering with his dominion.

She would not tell him he was beautiful when he was mad. She would not. Even if he was.

"Cerberus, find her a room. A nice one, not a cell." Hades turned on his heel and walked away, his broad back and tight buttocks flexing. Not that she noticed. Much.

She frowned, as his words hit her. Wait a minute. "Hey. What am I supposed to do sitting around here?"

He glanced over his shoulder at her. "I can give you hundreds of suggestions, bit, but they'd all involve you being naked again."

Sounds goo...bad. Very, very bad. She bared her teeth at his deliberate crudeness. "I'm serious."

"As am I. No? Fine, then, you can do what the Olympians do best...twiddle your thumbs while I handle the problem."

That arrogant horse's ass. She watched him leave, wishing she had the courage to say it out loud, but she wasn't about to pit herself against the Lord of the Underworld any more than she already had. She couldn't help herself from sticking out her tongue at his cursed, sexy back though.

Which she promptly pulled back in, shocked, when she felt the phantom brush of an invisible tongue against hers. His laughter echoed down the hall back to her.

3

Persephone didn't know what she should gape at first, her once-in-a-lifetime chance to view the palace of the Lord of the Underworld or the three-headed dog leading her through the maze of stairs and hallways.

"Do you like to throw balls?"

She blinked at the tawny head, the first words the creature had spoken directly to her. "I beg your pardon?"

It turned to her. The other two heads stared grimly ahead, though she thought she saw the white one roll its eyes.

"Throwing? Not just balls. Sticks will do too. I do. Well, I like to catch stuff. I can't throw much because I have no opposable thumbs, but I do so love to catch things that other people, that is, the master, will throw. Sometimes he throws fireballs, and then we get to catch them, though they make my breath smell after, the master says—"

"Silence," the middle head growled.

Cowed, the chatty head lowered. It cast her a sideways glance, sorrow in its gaze. "Sorry."

She would not feel bad for a hellhound. She would not feel bad for a hellhound. She would not...

"I thought you guarded the entrance to the Underworld," she said after an uncomfortable silence.

The middle head grunted. "Cerberus does."

Oh, that cleared things up. Not. "Isn't that you?"

The tawny head once again looked at her, its tongue hanging out of a doggy grin as if it was pleased as punch to be making conversation again. "Oh, there are lots of our kind, but we're the only ones the master allows in his palace. He loves us sooooo much. We're unique."

Middle head, who could easily have been a proper butler, gave a delicate snort. "You're the unique one."

"That's what master says. I'm the head that makes this Cerberus unique."

"You're lucky you didn't get us drowned upon creation."

Before tawny head could be chastened again, Persephone intervened. "And you're all called Cerberus?"

Tawny nodded. "That's our collective name. Though master calls me—only my head, because I'm special..." it shot a triumphant look at the others, "...Bob."

Okay. "I see. None of the rest of you have names?"

Middle head gave a put-upon sigh. "Our sire calls me Middle, and..." he indicated the eerily quiet white head staring straight ahead as they plodded, "...it is called Right."

Not a very imaginative guy, this Hades.

"You can call me Bob too, if you like, my lady."

"I'm not your lady."

"You are a deity," it said simply.

Barely. She didn't speak, but Bob had clearly decided that she was fine with its prattling, because it chattered nonstop. Its favorite topic of conversation, she discovered quickly, was Hades. "Do you like to scratch dogs' heads? My master scratches my head just right..."

"My master doesn't even get mad when I gnaw on the souls in Tartarus..."

"My master lets us sleep near him when I have a nightmare..."

"My master...my master...my master..."

She found it kind of endearing, actually, and wondered if this Cerberus really had been in danger of being destroyed when it became evident that Bob was not exactly the grim face of terror. If so, it was a point in Hades's favor that he hadn't done so—indeed, he even seemed to indulge the nonsensical creature.

Don't you go liking him just because he cares for a goofy dog.

They came to a halt in front of a set of double doors that flew open on its own. "This will be your room for the time being..." Middle began, and then stopped.

She waited for it to finish, but its gaze was focused on something behind her. Indeed, all six eyes were looking past her. "Cerberus?"

Bob craned its neck. "How'd you—? Ow." It frowned at Middle, who had knocked their heads together. "What?"

Middle ignored it. "My lady. I hope your room pleases you." It dipped its head and stood to the side to allow her entrance.

She entered and drew in a sharp breath. Scarlet-red curtains hung from a decadently large bed centered in the middle of the room. The rest of the furnishings were a dark brown—so dark they appeared black—while the floor was covered in a carpet that made her want to kick off her slippers and sink into it. It looked like a madam's room in a whorehouse.

She loved it. It was utterly different from her room at

home, which while pretty, looked girlish in comparison with its pastel floral décor. This was very clearly a woman's room.

If only it wasn't so devoid of natural light. There was a large alcove for a window, and a plush red velvet seat, but no actual glass. The light came from gas lamps scattered around the room.

"Thank you, Cerberus. This will do nicely."

"Is there anything else you require?"

Sunshine. Flowers. Home. Those thick arms— She cut off that thought. "I guess food or drink is out, huh?" Not that she needed food or water to survive, but she enjoyed it as a novelty and as a comfort, particularly if it was something she'd grown herself.

"We have both, but alas, those rumors are true. If you consume any food or drink in the Underworld, you remain in the Underworld."

Was that a hint of warning she heard? She turned to the hellhound. "How long will I be here?"

Middle inclined its head. "I will see if there is any news and come to you post-haste if there is."

"Thank you."

Its body took a step away, but Right spoke. She wasn't surprised to hear that its voice was rusty with disuse. "Have a care, lady. Bob may be foolish—"

"I am not."

"And Middle may be polite, but should you cross Lord Hades, neither will stop me from ripping off your limbs and feasting on them." Right flattened its lips and pulled them back so she could see its sharp canines and gums. Saliva dripped down to darken the white fur around its mouth.

She shivered as it stalked out, the door closing on Bob's chiding voice. "That wasn't very nice..."

Persephone chafed her arms with her hands as she

wandered around the room, finally sinking with a sigh onto the window seat. She hated this feeling. Would there ever come a time when she wouldn't feel like a particularly limp yo-yo, jerked from one world to the next?

"Hello, my little tulip."

She turned with a jerk at the loud, booming voice and focused on the apparition hovering in the middle of the room. "Zeus?" She hadn't seen Zeus in years, and then only for a brief time before she'd left Olympus, but he looked relaxed and hearty, his light brown hair long and flowing. He had grown facial hair since she had seen him last, a neatly trimmed Vandyke beard. His eyes were a matching light brown and danced with merriment, but Persephone knew they hid a ruthless and cunning mind. He wasn't completely solid; she could see the door through him. "Is that really you?"

"Of course."

Her eyes narrowed. She may not have spent a lot of time around gods, but she knew their trickery. This could very well be some plot of Hades. "Prove it."

"Oh, my suspicious rose. Okay. First time I met you, you were crying."

Of course she was crying—she'd been running from horny Hermes. Little winged bastard could flit around fast. That didn't prove Zeus's identity, as any number of people could have seen her or heard the story from him. Gods were a gossipy lot. "You need to do better than that."

He glowered. "Fine. Last time you saw me, *I* was crying."

Wincing in remembered sympathy, she smiled. "I'm sorry that nymph kicked you where she did."

"Trust me, so am I. Ugh. So this is how Hades decorates, huh? It's so garish." Zeus studied his surroundings with a small curl to his lip.

"It's not so bad." As she said the words, she wondered why she was defending that boor. To cover her slip, she rushed to speak. "I assume you've never been here then?"

"Nope. Hades forbids all of us from entering."

He sounded remarkably cheerful for someone who was breaking a massive rule. "So why are you here? For that matter, why am I here?"

"Well, I'm here—sort of here—to put some of your worries to rest. Don't have a lot of time, so I'm going to have to use my considerable soothing powers to calm you quickly."

His angelic countenance didn't fool her. "And why am I here?"

"Oh, that. I put you here."

THE THIRD TIME Cerberus cleared its throat, Hades poked his head out of his large walk-in closet. "What?" he snapped.

Only his demon dog would dare intrude upon him when he was in this mood. Middle spoke. "Sire, I merely wanted to assure you that Lady Persephone is settled nicely in the red room."

"Great, good." The red room, which happened to be next to his room. Not that that mattered—he had a better chance of fucking Medusa than he did Sephie.

Once again...not that that mattered.

"She is quite an interesting young lady."

He grunted, which shut up Middle, the very proper and conscientious head, but had no affect on Bob, who set the hound's tail to wagging in its eagerness. "Do you know what she's the goddess of, master?"

"No. And I don't care, as long as I can figure out who has

the giant balls to fuck with me." He found what he was looking for shoved into a corner on the bottom shelf of his closet, and he grabbed it.

There was only one person he could think of who had the aforementioned testicles, the absolute gall, to tamper with his life. He pulled the silk wrapping off the large glass sphere and thunked the priceless artifact on his desk. "Zeus!" he yelled. "You bloody git. I want to talk to you."

The black surface shimmered and then began to swirl, galaxies drifting across it, until a face he hadn't seen in centuries—which wasn't long enough—appeared. "Is that any way to talk to your brother?"

"It is when I've been cursed with you."

"Tsk, tsk. That world you live in has completely stripped you of all pleasantries. Here, let me help. Hello, Hades. How have you been? It's been, what, a few hundred years?"

"Cut that out. I want to know one thing and one thing only...did you send this Persephone to me? Are you preventing me from sending her out of here?"

"Yes and yes."

Hades opened his mouth and closed it, completely unprepared for that fast and calm *mea culpa*. "I... What?"

"Hear me out, Hades. She's in danger. I had no choice."

Hades dropped into his chair. "Make this fast."

"I discovered a bit of a, shall we say, wager amongst some of the younger gods."

"With Persephone as what, the prize?"

"Well, yes. You know how they are." Zeus laughed. "We were like that once, all full of boasting and competition."

Zeus and Poseidon had been. Hades had never been young, and he sure as hell hadn't been chasing after unwilling women. "Since when do you care about some other deity, Zeus?"

"You wound me. Though you're right, normally I'd be all for chasing a maiden, but Persephone has a power that is much needed by the humans, and I couldn't risk that she be damaged. You see, the competition wasn't just to woo her...but to take her."

Take her? Hades blood started to simmer. "Take her how?"

Zeus made a face. And if anything-goes Zeus was making a face, it must not have been pretty. "You know."

"Assault her."

He nodded reluctantly. "Yes."

Hades cracked his knuckles. "I want names." All that soft, supple flesh, that delightful spark of spirit that had defied him so boldly, crushed beneath the heels of some renegade gods? Not a chance.

"Relax, brother. I'm sorting it all out. Give me a little time to take care of these fools."

"And how are you going to take care of them? A slap on the wrist? Gods will be Gods?"

Zeus's face twisted, his light eyes going dark, and in them Hades saw his brother's true, endless power. "More than a slap," the god breathed.

Hades subsided, mollified.

Zeus turned cheerful again in a snap. "In the interim, shelter Persephone down there, would you?"

Keep her with him? That wasn't a hardship. He had had far less attractive and tempting morsels in his private abode.

She won't see it that way.

No, she would be scared and terrified of the thought of being trapped with him, even if it saved her. Hell, to her, he probably was the fate worse than death.

"Hey, Hades, you there?" Zeus was snapping his fingers.

He jerked to attention. "Fine. I'll keep her."

"Keep? Now, be careful. Persephone may be a good-looking piece but don't go getting any ideas about trying to steal her away from us. She's pretty vital to the Earth and the mortals." Zeus's hearty laugh couldn't hide the flash of warning in his eyes.

The unspoken threat raised Hades's hackles. He bared his teeth. "I wouldn't dream of it. I have a few terms for you, though. Remove the block that kept me from sending her back and tell me how you managed to get her past my shield." Every security system had vulnerabilities, but he made his as close to impenetrable as possible. Besides, no one in any world would get away with making a mockery of his powers.

Zeus frowned. "I'm sorry, did you say something?" The picture faded in and out rapidly. "You're...cutting...out..."

"Son of a bitch, Zeus, don't you dare..."

"I'll give you a ring when it's all clear on this end. Toodles."

"Zeus—" Too late. The ball went black, and Hades knew the other god wouldn't answer again until he was good and ready.

Only the clearing of Middle's throat stopped him from hurling the sphere against the wall. He tried to control his temper around his servants, not that he often succeeded.

"Sire, what is the plan then?"

"She stays." Damn it, his body certainly liked that idea.

"Shall I tell my lady?"

He hesitated. He really ought to let Cerberus go and inform her, but that perverse, irritating part of him that couldn't stop himself from being interested in the unattainable roared to life. He stood. "No. I'll take care of it."

"Very good, sire. Um. Might I be so bold as to warn you to watch out for the flowers?"

4

Hades understood Cerberus's cryptic words when he neared the red room. A long vine sprouting the most unusual flowers snaked along the granite floor. He knelt and touched the petal of a bloom, finding it velvety smooth and warm, as if it had sprouted from the ground in some sun-drenched garden and not from the stone floor of his palace.

He plucked the flower and held it to his nose. There. It was Persephone's scent.

The sharp punctures. Thorns. She'd manifested poking him with a thousand thorns when she was sitting on his lap. Seemingly without even being aware of it.

Fascinating.

He rose and tucked the flower into the pocket of his pants. Intrigued, he followed the vegetation all the way to where it disappeared, sure enough, under the door of the red room. Was this his new visitor's version of a trail of breadcrumbs?

He grasped the doorknob and was about to push it open when he had second thoughts. *Knock first.* That was what

Hot as Hades   31

civilized people did, right? Before he could call himself a fool, he gave two rapid knocks to the heavy wood. It was rewarded, to his surprise, by a meek, "Come in."

He shoved the door open and raised a brow. Had he thought the vine odd? It was nothing compared to the tropically scented paradise that had bloomed in Persephone's room. Plants of all kinds had sprouted, seemingly from the walls and floors, wrapping around the four posts of the bed, entwining with the gas chandelier. Most were flower bearing, bringing bursts of greens and pinks and blues and yellows. The unusual rainbow profusion was a reminder of the stark colors of his world.

In the center of this new garden sat Persephone, curled up with her back to him on the window seat, chin in her hand. Had there been a window there, she would have been gazing out of it. As it was, she was staring at a black wall, her profile in sharp relief. "Did you bring me news, Cerberus?"

Ah. She assumed he was his manservant. That explained her relaxed posture. For the first time he wished his body, glorious as it was, was really a three-headed dog, if that put her at ease. "It is I. And yes, I have news."

His voice made her back stiffen—with loathing he presumed—and she straightened and half turned to look at him. He held up his hand to stop her from scrambling to stand. "Please sit."

She subsided back in her seat and stared at him, eyes big and haunting, so fresh and lovely it made his back teeth ache with want. Unable to speak and look at her at the same time, he focused on a point over her left shoulder. "I spoke with Zeus. He said..."

"That he was the one who sent me here. I know." Her tone was flat.

His never-ending suspicion niggled. "How do you know?"

"He came to me, was standing where you are now."

Hades checked the urge to move away from the spot. "He was here bodily?"

"No. He was translucent."

That was something, he supposed, but if Zeus had managed to send Persephone a shade of himself here, it wouldn't be any great hardship to send his corporeal self here eventually. That wouldn't be tolerated. Hades liked to limit his involvement in cosmic showdowns, and Zeus showing up would certainly result in the blowing up of at least one universe. *Note to self: prioritize revamping security system.*

But first, he had to handle his guest. "And you know why he sent you?"

"Yes."

"You're taking the news pretty well." There were no tears or disbelief or anger or accusations of fabrication.

She curled her legs beneath her, her skirt making a waterfall off the seat. "Trust me, this is nothing new."

He took advantage of her sudden lack of hostility to probe further. "The gods often try to hurt you?"

"Yes. You see, I'm easy."

"Ah. Ahem." He cleared his throat, taken aback by her candor. He should probably let this lie, but he'd seen enough of the ugliness of humanity to let her believe that she was at fault here. "Like the nymphos. I wouldn't call them easy so much as generous, and even if you are generous, that's no excuse for them to chase you against your will—"

Did he imagine the twitch of her lips? "No. I mean, I may

be a goddess, but I was raised by mortals, and Demeter has only had time to develop the powers of mine that are most necessary to the world and to her. The other gods know this. I'm an easy target." She turned back to the faux window and propped her chin in her hand. A new tendril broke off from the vine nearest her head and slowly unfurled until it was long enough to drape over her shoulders, as if it were giving her a hug.

"I see." No wonder she couldn't materialize clothes or break free of bonds on command. Despite her well of power, she had no idea how to manipulate it. Most gods with powers that deep were taught early on exactly what they could do with them. "What, ah..." He sidestepped a vine that was slithering toward his ankle. "What exactly are you the goddess of?"

"Vegetation."

Demeter, you smart cookie. His cold and self-serving sister wasn't the type to adopt orphans unless something was in it for her. Demeter was the goddess of the harvest, so Persephone's untapped power would amplify hers.

"I know. You don't have to say it." Persephone faced him again and shook her head. "Aphrodite has beauty and Artemis has war and Athena has wisdom, and what do I have?" She flung her arms wide, as if to encompass the room. "A green thumb. Useless, I tell you."

"Well. I wouldn't say that." Oh dear gods, were her eyes wet with tears? No, no. Give him a screaming woman over a crying one any day of the week. He looked around the room at the sudden greenhouse. "Vegetation is...important. Especially to humans. They are weak soft creatures who require oxygen. Also they are highly anxious and plants are nice to look at. Very important for their morale. "

"I'm sorry about all this growth. I do it subconsciously when I'm upset or sad or mad... I can't help it." Persephone wiped at her eyes. "If I was stronger, Zeus wouldn't have even been able to fling me down here without my consent."

Privately, he disagreed with her. Over the years his powers had grown in leaps and bounds. Though he didn't keep extremely close tabs on all of the original six, he assumed theirs had as well. Even if she did tap into all her powers, she'd probably be no match for Zeus. Not really.

Her loud sniff brought him back to the here and now. Panic crept up his throat. He needed to get away before she broke down. He could not remember the last time he'd cried, and he had no experience with such an emotion. Or any emotion, rather. "I'm going to... I should go do some work."

She seemed to shrink. "Of course. I'm sorry for being such a bother."

"It's fine."

"I know now that you had no say in any of this. I apologize for screeching at you earlier, and for accusing you of all sorts of horrible stuff."

So few beings ever showed him gratitude or remorse. He scratched at his chest. He didn't get hives. Why was he so itchy? "That's okay."

"No, it's not." She peered up at him, all earnest and sweet. "It's kind of you to help me."

He resisted the urge to claw at his skin. "No one's ever accused me of being kind."

"You're letting me stay in your home."

What was this soft, kind tone in her voice? Why was it being directed at him?

He didn't want her spitting venom at him, exactly...but venom he understood. Gratitude and understanding, he did not. "I have no choice," he reminded her brutally. "Zeus has prohibited me from sending you back, remember?"

"You could kill me."

The words lay between them, heavy and stark. She rose from her seat and sauntered over to him. Her golden-brown skin gleamed in the firelight, her eyes too smart as they searched his face. "Why didn't you kill me, Hades?"

His hands clenched at his sides, a move that didn't go unnoticed by her. Let her think he was trying to keep from wringing her neck, and not the truth—he was trying to keep from stroking that soft skin. "The option is still on the table."

Her lips curved. "No, it's not, or you would have done it already."

Damn her. "Listen, goddess. Don't go getting any kind of romanticized notions about me, got it?" He stalked closer, until they were nose to nose. Or nose to chest—he had to lean down to truly look her in the eyes. He considered shrinking his form, but his vanity wouldn't really allow that.

Bigger, badder creatures than she had backed away when confronted with his gaze. Not her. She met it, confusing and angering and, hell yes, arousing him. "I'm not romanticizing anything. I'm simply thanking you for giving me sanctuary."

"I could still kill you, you know." He hated that he sounded like a whining, petulant child.

"I'll keep that in mind." Her face was sober, but he knew he wasn't imagining the laughter in her tone. How had she flipped from fear to gentle teasing so fast? "I promise I'll keep out of your way while I'm here."

"Good. You...do that."

"I will."

"Good."

"You already said that."

Hades stared at her. He fucking hated feeling confused. He also hated to not have the last word. "Just...stay. In your room." He turned and stalked out of the room before he could make a greater fool of himself.

5

She didn't stay.

For the next week, Persephone seemed to be everywhere and anywhere in his palace. A typical goddess might have lazed around in her luxurious room, but of course he got an industrious, bustling woman. He learned from Bob, who she'd taken a liking to, much to the disgust of Cerberus's other two heads, that at home she often worked in her gardens from sunup until sundown.

Since his palace floated in the Underworld, he had no garden or sun, but it didn't take long for Persephone to scurry around his home as if she owned it. He couldn't get away from her. He found her studying the books in his library, polishing silver in his dining room, leaving the baths clad in a damp robe, wet and sultry from the heat. She always greeted him with a warm smile and tried to converse with him as if he were a normal god and not the terror of godlings everywhere. When she wasn't around, her damn flowers and her scent filled the room.

Despite their close quarters, he did his best to avoid talking to her, which if he wasn't mistaken only increased their run-ins and made her more determined to chatter at him. He responded with grunts and one-word sentences and stalked away as quickly as possible. Any more interaction and he feared he would rip her dress off and throw her to the ground. Or press her up against the wall. Or toss her on the table. Or...really, any flat surface was fair game.

His fingers literally itched when he was around her. Never had he felt so utterly driven to possess a woman, one he was fully aware was off limits. Fuck her when she was a vulnerable guest in his home? That might enhance his already fearsome reputation, but he wasn't going to go around feeling like a bastard. No thanks.

So it was understandable why he found himself creeping like a criminal in his own palace one morning. *I should lock her up*, he thought grimly as he stuck to the shadows of the hall, ears perked for the soft shuffle of feminine slippers or her lilting laugh as she chatted with Bob. He considered confining her to her room about twelve times every day. Keep her in one place so he'd never have to see her beautiful face or smell those fucking flowers that followed her everywhere or hear her laughter ringing through his stark, silent halls. It was still a possibility.

Liar.

Fine. Maybe it wasn't.

He made it to his office and almost breathed a sigh of relief. That is until he opened the door and found her sitting in his chair—*his* chair—sorting through the papers on his desk. Her hair was dark and shiny, pinned up to reveal the nape of her neck, and she wore one of the many dresses he'd conjured into her closet. This one was black silk, a corset top that pushed her breasts up and over the rough lace neckline. He imagined her nipples peeking through that lace, as he had when he'd conjured it up, and his body instantly hardened.

He was going to die of blue balls before Zeus got this goddess out of here. He should have materialized some nuns' habits for her.

Pent-up lust and frustration had him snapping, "What the hell are you doing?"

He was gratified that she at least jumped. "Oh. Hello. Um, I was bored, so I thought I would try to help you by organizing some of your papers."

His papers were organized. He had a system. A very complex, messy-to-everyone-else-but-understandable-only-to-him system. He stalked over, prepared to be irritated.

But then she looked at him, and her look knocked the bluster out of him and made him want to fall to his knees in front of her—or, alternatively, have her on her knees in front of him.

He snarled, and she shrank back, though it was directed at him, not her.

"I didn't mean to make you mad. I thought I could be useful."

And being useful was, for some reason, important to her. Resigned, he knew that he wouldn't be able to blow up at her over the papers on his desk, now sorted in neat piles, probably alphabetized. "It's fine," he heard himself say. And though he choked on it a little, he lied. "Thanks. I appreciate your help."

She beamed as she pushed back her chair and stood. "You're welcome. Is there anything else I can do for you?"

He was fairly certain that "fellatio" was not the answer she was looking for. "No, not at the moment."

"Um. Okay, then. I guess I'll go back to my room and read for a while." She leaned forward, and for a second he wondered if she was going to kiss him. Her face came closer, and her hair tickled his nose. But no, she leaned past him and picked up the heretofore unnoticed book on his desk. He could see it was one of the primers that godlings used to develop their powers.

Though he knew he should let her go, her nearness screwed with his brain cells because he found himself initiating conversation. "I see you've found something to read in my library."

Her cheeks flushed a becoming shade of pink. "I know it's a book for children, but I'm usually working too much when I'm home to have time to read. We don't have a big library anyway." Her tone was defensive.

"I'm not making fun of you." He made a note to obtain some more primers and place them in the library in an easy-to-see place. He didn't want to embarrass her by handing them to her. "Have you learned anything?"

"Yes. Look." She caught her tongue between her teeth and took on a look of intense concentration. The door to the study slowly swung shut. She let out a little whoop. "Did you see that? I could never do telekinesis at all before."

Such a simple skill for those of their power, yet she looked as proud as if she'd walked on water. He'd forgotten what it felt like to have pride in accomplishing something so minor. Her excitement was contagious, and he found himself smiling. "Well done."

Her grin was rueful. "You probably think I'm silly."

"Not at all. Everyone has to start somewhere."

"I have a long way to go."

The self-deprecation in her voice bothered him on some basic level he didn't care to analyze. "You'll get there."

"I wish I could speed it up. I'd do anything to feel not so weak anymore."

Walk away. Her vulnerability had him rooted to the spot, though. "You aren't weak," he blurted out. *Not your business.*

"What?"

"You aren't weak."

"You don't know that."

He shifted his weight. "I told you, I can see what's inside. Granted, it works differently with other deities than it does with mortals—I can't see your whole past—but I can see that you're filled with power. And when you have power, when you can harness and use that power, you're always strong."

Her little button nose crinkled. "I guess that's my problem. No idea how to really do anything. Maybe my trip here had a greater purpose—time to study."

Trip? She made it sound like the Underworld was a fancy spa. "Studying will only give you a theoretical understanding. You need to be properly trained." *Go away now.* But she was talking to him! And looking at him without fear! "I could help you." *Shut up. Shut up. Shut up.*

"You could...what?"

Oh, what the fuck. "You just need a little training, bit. I could, maybe, you know. Help. If you want." *Shut. Up.* Because training meant that he'd be with her. Close to her. He wouldn't be able to skulk about, hiding from her, and he wouldn't be able to refuse to converse with her. Not when he was training her. He'd be confronted with her enticing curves at every opportunity.

"Surely you have a kingdom to run."

"Yes. Souls to torture, flesh to flay. But I delegate really well."

She gave no outward reaction to his flip words. "And what would you get out of this?"

Smart girl. No god ever did anything for free. It was

hard-wired into their kind. By all rights, he should have been writhing in agony over this one-sided transaction.

Technically, though, he supposed training her did give a nice little eff you to all those spoiled pansies at Olympus. If he did his job properly, and if she was an apt pupil, she would be able to really ruin any god who tried to put their hands on her. Wasn't screwing with Olympians payment enough? "The satisfaction of a good deed?" Her snort made him smile. "I swear, I demand nothing from you."

"Not even sex?"

The words fell between them like shards of ice. "I do not bargain for fucking, lady," he said softly.

His tone seemed to fluster her. "I wasn't implying that you were. I..."

"Forget my offer." He turned his back on her and stalked to the door. Goddamn it, when would he be able to get away from his damnable reputation? And why did he care that she thought the worst of him, like everyone else on Earth and in Heaven?

"Wait. Damn it, Hades. What if I want to have sex with you?"

He stopped short and turned to face her. "What?"

Her cheeks were so red, he wondered if the blush hurt her.

"I...I didn't mean to blurt that out..."

"You want to fuck?"

"Well, no, not at the moment I don't." She glared at him. "Especially when you put it in such flowery language as that."

"I'm not a flowery god. I'm simple. So you need to be simple back. Do you want to fuck?"

"I... Maybe."

"I despise coyness."

Hot as Hades 43

"I'm not trying to be coy," she snapped. "I'm trying to figure out my own feelings, and I'm embarrassed by frank talk."

"The other gods wouldn't be."

"I'm not like the other gods."

Thank the heavens. Neither was he. Yet he couldn't really blame her for having a suspicious attitude toward him, could he? The emotion was ingrained in every deity, even the atypical ones. "I don't want you to have sex with me because you're feeling grateful or some shit."

She nibbled her lower lip. "It's not that."

Yet he couldn't quite believe her. Though his body screamed at him to take whatever sexual crumbs she offered, that wasn't in his nature. He walked back over to her and held out his hand. "You want to be trained by me or not?"

She hesitated, but then took his hand. "I would be honored."

He let his hand warm, not letting her go when she gasped. "I, Hades, Lord of the Underworld, vow to train you to the best of my abilities. I will ask nothing in return except that you learn as well as you can and use the powers as you deem best fitting."

"How pretty."

"Wait, I'm not finished. Any boons or favors you grant me will be of your own free will, because you truly desire me, and not because you feel motivated by anything other than lust or sexual need. I will make no overtures toward you until such a time." He leaned closer, until they were nose to nose. "I think that takes care of both of our concerns, doesn't it?"

"It's sad we can't trust each other."

It was. "That's the way it goes amongst our kind, bit."

She huffed a small breath. "Fine. I agree to everything." A small pulse of magic went through both of them until a black lock floated above their joined hands.

He released her earlier than he wanted to, mainly because the feel of her small fingers in his made him want to suck on them. "There. Done." Pivoting on his heel, he walked back to the door.

"Hades."

He hadn't realized she was so close, that she'd followed him. He turned at the threshold of the door, looking down at her as she stood there. She was so short compared to him. He wanted to pick her up and put her in his pocket. "Yes?"

"When do we start?"

For a second, he wondered if she was talking about the sex or the training. No, it must be the training. "Tomorrow morning. Be in my gym as soon as you wake."

"I'll see you then."

That was such a pleasant threat, he didn't realize until he was in his bedroom that she'd essentially ushered him out of his own office.

6

"Concentrate."

Persephone was starting to hate that word, at least when it was uttered in Hades' superior tone. She'd heard it a lot over the past week. "I am concentrating."

"No, you aren't."

Persephone gritted her teeth as she stared at the knife hovering in mid-air. Hades had decided to start at basics, with her telekinesis ability, or what she had of it. At least the knife wasn't wobbling too badly as it neared the bulls-eye he'd conjured. The sharp tip bounced against the red dot in the center and clattered to the floor. "Curses," she whispered.

"You need to—"

"Concentrate. I know. I'm trying." She rolled her shoulders.

"I was going to say you need to relax." Hades lifted his hand, and the knife zipped over to him without a second's delay.

Showoff. "Tossing knives around isn't how I relax at home."

He eyed her skeptically. "You seem far too industrious to ever relax."

That, she acknowledged. Demeter had drummed the importance of hard work into her, and tending to the human land did require much work. "I like to wind down with some music and a book."

He grunted and waved his hand. A large red screen appeared above their heads, hovering in the air, filled with black symbols that scanned back and forth faster than she could make sense of them.

"What on earth is that?"

His endless eyes squinted, but he didn't answer. He swiped his hand and the symbols moved faster. They made up a language, perhaps, but one that was far too ancient for her to understand. "Ah-ha. That's where I put them. Cerberus!"

The creature immediately padded into the room, as if it was hovering on call, which it most definitely was. "You rang, master?"

"These musicians, in the pits. Bring them here."

"Yes. As you wish, master." Cerberus padded out.

"What are you doing?"

"Bringing you music."

Persephone held up her hands. "I don't want you to bring poor souls up here and torture them by forcing them to play for me."

"It will be the least of the torture they've undergone since they've died. Might actually be a nice break for them."

She frowned. "I won't be a part of hurting anyone."

His jaw flexed. He swiped his hand again, and the symbols morphed into a language she could read. "The first soul you're so worried about, when he was mortal, he skinned his wife and children alive."

Hot as Hades

She recoiled from the detailed description of the crime on the hovering screen.

He swiped, and another dossier filled the screen. "This one was a key member of a genocidal dictator's political party." Another swipe. "This trombone player..." Hades squinted.

"Purchased a vanity license plate that read NiceBrass," Persephone read out loud. "Tacky, but that sin warrants a *pit*, Lord Hades?"

"Um..." Hades scrolled down, then let out a breath. "No, no, he also set dozens of houses on fire. What a relief, I thought there might be a glitch in the system."

"Yes, that's quite a relief," Persephone said dryly. Before she could continue, three haggard looking souls flashed into the room. Upon spying Hades, they immediately fell to their knees, sobbing and begging.

"Silence," he roared, and she jumped, though it wasn't directed at her. The souls stopped like he'd muzzled them, and perhaps he had. They all suddenly had instruments in their hands, and he nodded. "Play."

She blinked in bemusement as music filled the room. It wasn't calming music, but it was music.

He stalked closer. "Are you relaxed yet?" Hades demanded.

She controlled the twitch of her lips. "A little."

"Good. Then go." He tossed the knife up, caught it by the hilt, then flung it at the musicians.

Without consciously thinking, she raised her hands, and two thick streams of ivy shot out. One batted the knife aside as if it were a paper airplane, while the other wrapped around the startled souls, shielding them as they continued to play.

Her heart was pounding loud enough to wake the dead.

"What did I just do? I've never been able to control them like that. The vines usually just sprout and have a mind of their own."

He scratched at his jaw. "I don't know. Never seen anyone do something like that before."

The two of them looked at the knife on the floor. The ivy rolled into a ball and disappeared.

"Is that good?" she asked.

"Of course. You always make your power your bitch, twist it to suit your needs. Well done."

She bet Hades didn't praise much, so she hugged the words close. "Thank you."

With a wave of his hand, the trembling souls disappeared. "On that note, let's call it a day, shall we?"

"Already?"

"You've been at it for a while. I should probably check in on how my realm's being run."

"Souls to flay."

"Only the ones who deserve it." He gifted her with one of those slow, pulse-pounding smiles that made her entire stomach clench. She welcomed those smiles, had learned to appreciate their unusual appearance over the past couple of weeks of close contact. He might be scary, yes, but he was fair to a fault. He worked her hard, but she liked that. It meant that despite his chauvinistic smack talk, he didn't see her as less of a deity because she was a woman or untrained.

The sexual attraction between them continued to flourish. Not because of anything he said or did. He only had to strut around bare-chested and look at her in a certain way, and her body became flushed. She knew he was similarly affected by his sudden gruffness when she ventured too close, but he had kept to his promise that he wouldn't make any moves on her.

Foolish promise.

Every night, after hours of Hades trying to train her, as she lay alone in her gaudy bed, she considered the pros and cons of getting into a physical relationship with the Dark One. He was the first god, possibly ever, who made her want to toss her dress up and spread her legs.

Granted, he was still Hades, the Lord of the Underworld. But he wasn't nearly as bad as she'd been led to believe. And even if this was just a supremely awesome act he was putting on, what could a little bit of lustful release really hurt? The other deities coupled with barely a thought. Why couldn't the two of them do the same? She'd be leaving, as soon as Zeus gave the all clear, and she'd never see Hades again. He didn't leave his world, and she would learn how to control her own power so no one would be able to force her into any place she didn't wish to go to again.

Damn it all, yes. She would do this. She was strong, and independent, and she would take what she wanted and everyone else could go to hell. Another hell.

"Hades," she blurted out. He glanced at her, and her nerve took a prompt nosedive. "There's something else that helps me relax."

"What's that?"

"A bath."

He stilled. "No river in the castle, but you can use the hot springs."

"I know. Can you show me how to get there? I always lose my way."

Hades nodded. "Come."

She followed him out of the gym and through the criss-crossing hallways to the baths. She used the walking time to try to pump herself up again. Her confidence was only about forty-seven percent inflated when they reached their destination and Hades opened the door.

Filled with hot waterfalls and streams, the baths were her favorite place in this entire castle. The humidity stretched out to embrace her as she stepped inside and turned to face Hades. She didn't understand his amused smile until he tugged a flower from her hair.

She sighed. "Sorry. My mind wandered."

"That's fine. My servants are delighting in all of the fresh flowers they can arrange around the place." She grinned, since she'd noticed the familiar blooms stuffed in vases on hall tables.

His smile disappeared, his gaze intent upon her mouth, and she felt warmer than the steam accounted for. Her tongue crept out to lick her lips, and his eyes turned slumberous before he took a deep breath. "I should—"

"Don't."

"—go. What?"

Persephone inhaled. "Stay."

He scrutinized her. "You are aware of what would go down if I stayed, right?"

"I'm no innocent, Hades."

He crossed his arms over his bare chest. The muscles in his forearms flexed. "Why now?"

She was abruptly sick of all the constant questions and suspicions. Damn it, couldn't they, for once, forget they were two immortal deities and fuck? "Look, either stay or go. I don't care." *Liar.* "I'm not going to beg."

"I'm not asking for begging, but I made a formal binding vow not to touch you unless you asked for it, remember? You need to spell it out or I'm stuck, it pains me to say."

Pains, hell. The unholy light in his eyes told her that he was enjoying making her squirm. "I want to have sex with you, for no other reason than the needs of my flesh. I freely offer you my body. Good enough?"

It was like an invisible chain was cut, and he stepped forward, crowding her back into the room. The door swung shut behind him. "Perfect."

She swallowed. "Unless you have something more pressing to do, of course."

His hand smoothed down his bare chest with no self-consciousness and palmed the heavy length of his erection, now visible under his black trousers. "Trust me, this has been pressing for days."

Since he'd called her attention to it, she couldn't tear her gaze away from that bulge rapidly lengthening under the stroke of his hand. He groaned as she watched him. "Do you want to see me?"

"Yes."

"Then undress me."

She moved to unbutton his pants, but he stayed her hand. "No. Use your power."

Materializing and dematerializing objects was hard for her, and even harder when steam from the baths was curling around her from outside while the heat of her arousal made her internal temperature rise.

Closing her eyes, she concentrated. In a second, she heard him make a rough noise, and the steam was touching her bare skin. She glanced down at her naked body. "I didn't mean to strip myself."

"No. But I did."

She looked at him and caught her breath. He was naked except for the gold armbands wrapped around his bulging biceps. She could finally see where his tattoo ended, the serpent's tail flicking against and calling attention to his groin. His penis rose thick and long and curved from a tangle of dark hair, his balls hanging heavy beneath. When she combined his physical appearance with the intent expression he wore, he looked like a primitive conqueror. And she was lucky enough to be his conquest.

He stroked his cock as if he were teasing her, offering it to her, rubbing it up and down, smoothing his palm over the wet tip and using the lubrication to ease the rest of his way. Unable to keep herself from participating, she drew closer and grasped the length of the shaft, taking over the job from him. His hand wrapped around hers for the first few strokes, showing her how he liked it. She picked up his rhythm quickly, and he released her to exact his own delicious torture.

Her fist tightened involuntarily on him when he rubbed his thumb over her nipple, and he groaned, hastily removing her hand from him. "Did I hurt you?"

"No. Need to concentrate," he muttered. He stepped closer, leaned down and replaced his hand with his mouth. The pleasure was a sharp, shooting, almost pain straight to her pussy.

"How do you taste so good?" he asked, slurring the words against her breast, as if he were drunk on her.

Her hands passed over his shoulders and back, unable to find a grip on the slick play of flesh and muscle. "Hades..."

The next few seconds happened in a blur. He growled, the world spun, and she was pressed up against the wall. The stone was cold and hard against her back, while he was hot and hard against her front. Persephone tried to catch her breath as he stepped between her legs, his muscled hips stretching her thighs wide.

No chance. He gave her no time to adjust, simply bent his knees and pushed up inside of her. He fed her a few

Hot as Hades 53

inches and stopped when she squirmed on the end of his cock. "How does that feel?"

"So good." Better than good. The best she'd had and he hadn't even started thrusting. Some sense of self-preservation kept her from admitting that aloud.

Heat poured off him in waves, rivaling the steam of the baths, and he shoved inside of her harder, until she'd taken every inch of him. He barely gave her a chance to adjust before he was groaning, his hips thrusting, his flesh slapping against hers. He grasped her thighs and spread her legs wide so she was utterly open for his fucking, giving her no place to run or hide. His rhythm became wilder, less controlled, transforming into pure rutting.

He gave one last thrust and a rough groan, arching his back, until he was buried deep. Her pussy clenched down on him as he released inside of her.

Her thighs were still spread by his hands when his breathing slowed, evened out, and he withdrew. He took one look at her face and gave a slight groan. "Shit. I screwed that up, didn't I?"

She winced as she straightened her legs. The muscles felt wobbly and her knees weren't quite steady, so she braced one hand against his hard forearm and tried to control the trembling. "Not at all."

"You're lying again. You didn't even come."

Okay, maybe she was being a trifle disingenuous. It had been kind of fun to see Hades lose control and take her—*her*—like an animal in heat, but she could admit to some disappointment at her lack of orgasm. She would have liked to come. She would have really liked to come. In fact, she'd had sex with him in order to come. "So maybe it wasn't exactly the best sex I've ever had."

His brows slammed down over his eyes. "Is that a challenge?"

"What? No—"

"Because that was just the tip of my iceberg, baby."

How did his arrogance both turn her on and make her want to roll her eyes? "You were the one who said you screwed it up."

"And you agreed!"

All gods were crazy. "Listen..."

"No, you listen." With a flex of his muscles, he had her picked up in his arms. It felt good to lay against his chest naked. The last time it had happened, when she'd dropped into his lap, she'd been too confused and nervous to appreciate it. His arms were strong around her, and when she laid her head against his chest, she could hear the steady thump of his heart. "Not the best you've had..." he muttered in outrage. "We'll see about that."

Arguing any further seemed counterintuitive to the needs of her still-aching pussy. If he wanted to be her best lover, who was she to deny him?

Since they were in the baths and she hadn't yet taken one, she expected him to step with her into the heated water, but instead he lay her down on a soft, furry rug he must have materialized on the rock floor—it hadn't been in here before, that was for sure.

Curious and unappeased, she waited while he knelt between her legs and stared down at her body. His shaft was still hard, and the gas lamps in the room cast a smooth, burnished glow over his skin. He was utterly beautiful, with that big body and armbands and tattoo. She wanted to start at the top and lick her way down.

She reached for him, but he took her wrists and pinned them down at her sides. "No. This time I drive you crazy."

Hot as Hades

"I want to touch you."

"If you do, I'll be fucking you hard and fast again."

She grew wetter at the imagery. Really, she'd had no complaint with his technique, it had just been too short. She struggled against his hold, but no matter how much he'd trained her, in brute strength he was always going to be her superior.

That should have scared her, but it excited her in a primitive way. She could use her budding powers, she supposed...but she didn't want to.

"Hmmm," he said, glancing down at her pinned wrists. "I need to use my hands to drive you mad. Will you keep your hands here like a good girl?"

She nodded rapidly. "Yes."

"Don't move them."

"Okay."

He released her hands and spread her thighs farther so he could see up her entire body. And then...it might as well have been his hands that were captured because all he did was look. She didn't mind his long perusal of her breasts...she quite liked them, and by the glassy look in his eyes, she knew he did too. It was when he pushed her legs even farther apart and stared at her exposed pussy that she became uncomfortable. "Don't."

"Don't what?"

Forgetting her vow to keep her hands at her sides, she used one to cover up her mound. "Stop looking at me there."

He dragged his gaze up to hers, red fire flaring. "What did I say about your hands?" He pulled them away and stretched them above her head, leaving them there. When she gave an experimental tug, she realized he'd contained them with some sort of invisible tether.

Persephone inhaled and looked up at him. Wariness

briefly eclipsed the lust in his eyes. "If you want to stop, just tell me."

"I'm not scared of you." Well, she was, a little bit, but that uncertainty only made her more excited.

The fire flared darker, the wariness vanishing as he slipped back into the game. "You should be, little Sephie." He looked down idly at the place between her spread legs. "Why don't you like me looking at you here? You're beautiful, all wet and moist. I like a plump mons, and yours is nice and cushiony."

"It's private."

"Not for long. I'm going to know this pretty pink pussy better than you do by the time you..." Leave. The word was unsaid, but it hung between them.

She spoke, hoping to get them past the awkward moment. "Maybe we should bathe first?"

He continued to stroke her mound. "Why?"

"I'm a little messy."

"Mmm." Without warning, he slipped his finger inside of her. She gasped, watching the flex of his forearm as he thrust a second, and then a third finger inside of her, pumping rapidly. "Is that good?"

She shivered as he strummed those nerve endings back to life. "Yes."

"Better than my cock?"

"No." She arched her hips, trying to get closer, but perverse bastard that he was, Hades slowed his hand the more she struggled for it. "Hades."

As if he hadn't heard her, he withdrew slowly from her pussy, his eyes fixed on his fingers.

"You are messy, Sephie. You're so wet, and I shot all of that semen inside of you." He lifted his hand so she could see the glistening mix of his and her fluids on him. "I like to see you full of my come. Don't you?"

She nodded rapidly, ready to agree to anything to have some part of his body back inside of her. But he reached up and touched his hand to her lips, painting them with their fluids. "I like it so much, I may keep you filled with my come. Would you like that?"

"Yes," she sighed, her lips opening in an involuntary O when he carefully outlined them. He slipped his fingers inside of her mouth, and she closed around them, tasting both of them on his flesh.

His nostrils flared as he thrust the two fingers deeper, testing how far he could go with each push of his hand. With her hands tied, her options for seducing him into fucking her were limited, so she used her lips and teeth and tongue as best she could, sucking, licking, nibbling. He withdrew his fingers and dragged the wet digits over her mouth and chin to rest against the pulse beating in her throat. "Yeah. You'll drink my come, won't you, Sephie?"

"Oh yes."

He cupped his hands over her breasts and massaged them almost roughly. "And you'll wear it. I want to rub it into your skin, so I'm always on you, over you."

Anything. She would agree to anything. Had she thought she lusted for him before? It was nothing compared to the arousal strumming through her now.

"And here..." He smoothed both hands down her body until they were resting right above her pussy. "Here, I'll keep you filled all the time. Stuffed full of my cock."

"Yes, oh please, Hades."

"I love it when you say my name," he muttered as he grasped his penis and led it to her opening. "Gets me hard every time, Sephie."

He pushed inside of her, and they both gave a weighty sigh of relief. "How does that feel?"

He hit a particularly nice spot and she moaned. "Hard."

"Does that please you?"

"Yes."

"Do you want it longer?" To her shock, his cock lengthened inside her. "Thicker?"

She shrieked as he grew so big, every nerve ending flared to life. How...?

Because he was Hades. There was nothing he couldn't do. He literally had a magic dick.

He gave a dark chuckle. "Ah yes. That's the right size, isn't it? I'll remember. Keep you filled and screaming. For as long as you're here."

For as long as she was here. No, she wouldn't think of that, couldn't really think of anything.

She realized he'd freed her hands, and she wrapped her arms around him, doing the same with her legs, using her heels to goad his pistoning hips on. She orgasmed quickly, and he fucked her through it, triggering smaller though no less satisfying orgasms.

She came back to herself when he reached his satisfaction, his body arching over hers, a rough groan escaping his lips. The hot jets of his come bathed her pussy, and she flushed, remembering his words.

She stroked his back as he slumped over her. Being covered by Hades every day for eternity would be no hardship. Too bad she didn't have that long.

7

"**P**ersephone?"

"Yes?" She glanced up from where she was scratching Bob's head in front of the fire in the library. His hound was practically comatose in blissful happiness, its tongue hanging out in a doggy grin.

"I know we're supposed to train this morning, but I need to take care of some matters around my kingdom."

She frowned, her hand moving to Middle's ears. That head remained rigid for barely a second before it bowed slightly and slitted its eyes in pleasure as her nails dug in.

Persephone appeared particularly fetching today. Her hair was pulled back in a simple updo, the curls tumbling down her back while small wisps clung to her cheeks. She'd learned to materialize her own clothes, which was both a blessing and a curse. Today she wore a simple cotton frock of pink and white, and the innocence of the dress was more arousing than the velvet and silk and lace gowns he'd given her. Something barbaric in his brain liked the sham innocence covering that supple and inventive body.

Down, boy.

Every now and again he idly considered that maybe she was part of some larger illicit plot against him, then dismissed it. Though more than one ruler might have been toppled through sex, he was too tired of constantly suspecting everyone and everything. For now, he was going to enjoy this simple lust between them. Everything else could be sorted later.

"Where are you going?" she asked.

"I need to check in around the realm. I usually go out often, but..." He trailed off, unwilling to offer her so much power. *But you've utterly distracted me.*

"Can I come?"

He laughed before he realized she was serious. "You want to tour the Underworld?"

"Absolutely. This is a once-in-a-lifetime chance."

No. For the most part, the Underworld was a dangerous place. And hell, though he was keen on abandoning all suspicions, he found he couldn't quite turn off his reluctance to keep his world all to himself. "I don't know..."

"Please?"

She should patent that pleading look. "Persephone..."

Her hand moved to Right's head, and Hades tensed, ready to run to her rescue when the massive white beast mauled her. But as she petted it, the creature merely twisted around to lick her wrist. Then it turned to eye him. *Take her, fool,* it seemed to say. Still he hedged. "Well, I guess there are certain areas you could see. If you're sure—"

With a squeal, she jumped to her feet. "Yes, yes, let's *go.*"

"Okay then."

She gave each of Cerberus's heads a final pat and ran to grab his hand and tug him to his feet. Though he barely felt the pulls on his arm, he stood and allowed her to guide him

Hot as Hades 61

from the room, aware that she received pleasure from any display of physical superiority to him.

Hades cleared his throat. "You should have said you were this bored. You aren't a prisoner, you know."

She was practically dancing as they neared the front door. "I know. And I wasn't bored, exactly. I figured it probably wasn't smart to go wandering around a realm I don't know, and you're already giving me so much of your time, training me..."

"And fucking you," he added helpfully, giving a mock ouch when she pinched him. They stopped in front of the massive wooden door. "Seriously, you're absolutely right. There are parts of the kingdom that are downright dangerous, and I'd rather you not go out without me taking you to the safer areas."

"Will there be sunshine?"

The naked longing in her voice was unmistakable, and he kicked himself for not having thought of her needs sooner. Of course she missed sunshine—she was the goddess of plants, for fuck's sake. He was just now noticing the paleness of her formerly nut-brown skin.

He placed his hand on the door and called up the Elysian Fields, the perfect place for her to visit. "Yes." Opening the door, he watched the dawning joy on her face as the sunlight pierced his home. How had he not noticed how dark and cavernous his palace was?

They both had to squint as they stepped outside, so bright was the sunshine. The Elysian Fields was aptly named, resembling a huge park filled with green grass, large trees and the scent of sweet blooms. Persephone bent down to trace a rose, and the little flower stretched up toward her as if begging for her touch. She laughed, the sound tripping down his spine.

He cleared his throat. "Is this enough sunshine?"

She cast him a glowing smile and straightened. "Very much so. Are these the Elysian Fields?"

"Yes."

She looked around, and he knew she was absorbing everything. Persephone could have easily been a goddess of knowledge. She soaked in new experiences like a hungry sponge. He'd tutored her very little in actually using her powers. She'd grown by leaps and bounds all on her own.

"Then these people...are dead?"

He took his gaze off her and studied the souls packed on the greens. Their houses were some distance away, small cottages, large mega mansions and everything in between, since whatever they wanted, they received. They usually congregated here, however, for socializing and playing and simply soaking in the eternally perfect weather. "Yes. These are souls."

"I want to be sad, but they look so happy."

"They should be happy." Refusing to think of how natural it felt, he picked up her hand and put it on his arm. "They deserve it. See that man over there? He sacrificed himself to save fourteen other humans." He pointed to the other men around him who were laughing and slapping his back. "Three of those fourteen are here as well. They did great things with the lives he gave them."

"Wow."

"That lady, in the blue, she discovered a cure for a previously incurable disease. Killed herself in the process by breathing in chemicals, but she considered that worth it."

Persephone pointed to a couple sitting on a blanket. The women nuzzled each other and whispered. "What did they do?"

He cocked his head and studied them. "Ah. They fell in love, married, and had two children."

"So you can get here even if you do nothing amazing with your life?"

"Most of these souls did nothing amazing to get here. They simply lived. Some of them slipped up now and then, but on the whole, they were good people." He glanced around. "The majority of humans, they come here, actually."

"Slips don't get held against a soul?"

"I'm not the one who sorts the souls, but it doesn't seem that way. To err is human, after all. Like that guy? He cheated on his taxes a couple of times."

"You sound like you admire him."

He shrugged. "You know some mortals consider their tax collector scarier than Thanatos? It's damn insulting."

She reached up on her tiptoes and pecked his cheek. "Poor Hades."

He resisted the urge to place his hand over his cheek like a lovelorn calf. But when she looked away again, he stroked his fingers over his skin, savoring that casual sign of affection. "If you ever saw Death sulking about how he's not the *only* sure thing in a human's life, you wouldn't like taxes either."

She snorted. A child kicked a ball too hard and it came close to Hades. As the boy ran over, Hades gave the ball a gentle push with his foot. The child picked it up, looked through the two of them, and darted away. "Can they not see us?"

"No." He took a hold of her arm and led her farther down the path. "I carry my helm when I come here." He held his palm up, and a miniature black helm, about the size of a pebble, swirled in his hand. "It keeps me invisible. I cloaked you as well. I frighten them too much."

"Oh." She didn't say any more, but he could see the wheels in her awesome brain turning. "Does that...make you sad?"

Only in the beginning. Not anymore. He gave her a derisive look as he tucked the helm into his pocket. "Yes. It has me crying in my porridge that the itty-bitty souls are scared of me."

She rolled her eyes but thankfully shifted her attention to the beautiful scenery. The two of them took a turn about the park, just another couple strolling arm in arm. He wondered at the picture they would make if anyone could see him. She fit in here, small and lovely. He, big and scary and scowling, did not. When they came back to where they'd started, he reluctantly released her. "I actually do have to check on the other parts of the realm and speak with some of my servants. I'll drop you back off in the palace—"

"But I want to come."

"Sephie, trust me, this is pretty much the only nice place in the kingdom."

Her mouth set in that mulish line he recognized from when she badly wanted to get some task right and couldn't quite manage it. "I want to come."

"Persephone..."

"Hades." She raised that stubborn little chin and gave him one of her regal looks. How the hell did she manage to look down her nose at him when he was a full head taller than her? "Cloak my presence if you want, but I'm not going back to the palace. I want to come with you."

"But—"

"Unless..." She frowned. "Unless it's because you don't want another god to see your kingdom?"

"Not exactly," he hedged, and then threw his hands up in the air at her hurt expression. When had he become someone who cared about someone else's feelings? "Fine," he snapped. "Don't say I didn't warn you."

He grasped her hand and cast a portal to transport them. In a second, they were at the River Styx. "Keep this." He pressed the helm into her hand. "You're still invisible, but the thing also will cloak your powers, so yell if you need me," he told her, as she stared wide-eyed at the desperate, moaning souls lingering on the banks. "Now stay here while I talk to Charon. Bastard's been charging double what he's supposed to for his gimmicky ferry ride."

THIS HAD BEEN AN EYE-OPENING DAY. Persephone stood on a cliff in Tartarus, still cloaked in protection by Hades's invisibility spell. And thank the gods for it, as there were scary creatures and pain and fire everywhere she looked.

This was the true Underworld, the bowels of the realm that tainted the entire world with evil, that made others regard her Hades with fear.

Your Hades?

Well, for however long she would have him, yes. She glanced over at his powerful profile. She hadn't realized how relaxed he was with her now until she saw him slip into his cold, merciless mask to deal with his minions. It wasn't an easy job he had, to keep the scales of good and evil from tipping too much in one direction or another. A lesser god might have relaxed in his luxurious palace and delegated, but Hades appeared to be fully cognizant of his responsibilities as leader of this realm.

Her gaze slipped to the red-skinned, horned creature he

was currently viciously, verbally gutting. She feared it might move to a physical gutting soon, and her stomach was not strong enough to witness that.

A sudden movement caught her eye. Another devil, almost as large as Hades, crept up behind him. She'd watched Hades dressing the thing down earlier, noting the crazed fury in its eyes. It carried a pitchfork now, and like a time-lapse photo, she could see every frame of its body as it prepared to throw it. The lift of the sharp tip, the retraction of its shoulder, the fighting stance of its legs...

"Hades!" she yelled, but she was too far away, and other screams and yells drowned her out. In her panic, she tried to either still the thing's arm or deflect the spear somehow, but nothing happened, and she realized Hades's helm was blocking her powers. She started to run, stretching out a hand as if she could stop it, as the sharp object went airborne heading straight toward her guy. *No, no, no, no.*

A second later, Hades pivoted and held up his hands. What looked like a black rope thrust out of the ground and knocked the spear aside so it fell to the floor harmlessly, and then wrapped around the now- struggling devil. The creature was smashed against the hard rock wall, leaving a smear of black blood, and then flung off the cliff into the fiery pit.

When the black rope rolled up into a neat ball and disappeared, Persephone realized it hadn't been a rope at all.

It had been a vine.

Everyone had stopped what they were doing, and Hades seemed to grow larger before roaring, "Does anyone else wish to challenge me?"

Silence.

"Then get your asses back to work."

The din of screams and painful moans returned. Hades turned back to the devil he'd originally been speaking to. It nodded multiple times and scurried off. Had she not been watching Hades, she wouldn't have seen the slight bow to his shoulders and the sigh he gave before he straightened and marched toward her. "Walk," he muttered between his teeth.

When they turned a corner and were relatively isolated, he stopped them. "What did you do?"

"I...I have no idea. I couldn't get to you in time, and I was worried."

"A spear wouldn't have hurt me."

Of course it wouldn't have. She'd panicked. "I know. I'm not even sure how I... Have you been able to command plants before?"

"No." His mouth was grim. "You gave me your powers."

"I—" Terror bloomed. "I'm powerless now?"

"No. You gave me a shard of them. Somehow, even with the helm suppressing you."

That was a relief. "How? I didn't even know that was possible."

"Anything is possible. Doesn't mean I've ever heard of any gods actually doing it."

"Why not?"

His lips quirked. "Because we're all suspicious, selfish pricks, bit. We don't like to share anything."

"Oh." She thought about it. "I guess it doesn't really matter to me if you have some of my power. I mean, as long as I get to keep mine."

He studied her as if she were an odd species. "Yes. Even if you gave bits of your power out to every god, you'd still have an immeasurable amount."

"Okay then. Do you...feel any different?" *With a part of me inside of you?* The thought wasn't unpleasant.

"I feel...lighter? No, that's not the right word. I don't know if I can describe it." He stroked his hand over the stone wall of the cliff. Black tendrils sprouted from the harsh rock. Hades made a rough sound of surprise as the plant quickly covered the wall and started slithering to the ground.

"Controlling it isn't as easy as it looks, is it?"

He shot her a mock-dirty look. "I can control it fine." In a blink, the creeping plant had turned to ash. A gasp escaped her lips, and she placed her hands on her hips. "That wasn't nice. You can't burn the plants!"

"Sorry." He looked anything but repentant, though he finally sighed at her glare. "Okay, I won't do it again." A fierce look of concentration crossed his face, and he lifted his hand to the cliff again. This time, a single stalk grew, uncurling into a black rose. He plucked the flower once it was grown and handed it to her.

Charmed, she brought the unusual bloom to her nose to inhale its sweet fragrance. "Thank you. You're already more in control of my powers than I am."

His eyes narrowed. "Hmm." He turned and walked away, to the cliff. He stared down at the fire and steam below, glanced over his shoulder back at her, and then jumped.

"What the—" She sprinted to the edge. Her hands came up instinctually, thick green vines shooting out. This time, she was extremely conscious of what she was doing, and it was almost like the vegetation had senses just like she did. It took her a second to find him through the vision obscuring fire and brimstone, and then he was rising high above her, the plant wrapped around his middle.

The vines delivered him safely back on firm ground. He

stroked his hand over the greenery and she felt that stroke on her back. "It feels like satin," he marveled. "How is that so?"

She lifted her hand to her throat. This was too many adrenaline rushes in one day. "You said my powers were suppressed! Why would you risk that?"

"Clearly your powers are not suppressed, or you wouldn't have been able to give me a shard." He cocked his head. "I don't think anything in the universe could suppress you, 'Sephie."

She would not be distracted by that compliment. "I don't like these tricks."

"It wasn't a trick. It was a test. You seem to do best when you don't have time to get in your own head. Did you feel more in control?"

"Yes," she admitted, and glared at him. "It was still a trick."

He narrowed his gaze on her. "Are you tightening these binds on purpose?"

"Yes." She blinked, and elation shot through her. "Oh my. Yes! They're doing what I want them to."

A broad smile swept across his face, and his muscles flexed. The vines binding him dissolved, though not into ash this time. Oh no, they turned into hundreds of black butterflies. Delighted, she watched them flit into the air of the Underworld. "Oh Hades. You're remarkable."

He cleared his throat, and when she looked at him, his scowl was back. "Have you seen everything you wanted to see?"

"For one day, yes."

"I told you it wouldn't all be sunshine and flowers like the Fields." He opened a portal.

She stepped through, directly into the palace, and cast

him an arch look. "What made you think I expected that? Granted, I've been sheltered for most of my life, but I know there's bad out there. It needs to be dealt with, and it sucks that you're the one who has to do it, but probably better that you have the power, since you won't abuse it." She smiled and held up the flower he'd given her. "Besides, you're half wrong. Perhaps no sunshine, but you may have flowers in more places now."

He watched her, his face inscrutable, as she carefully tucked the rose into the pocket of her dress. "I have to go to my office," he said.

"Oh." Did he want to be alone? Had she said something wrong?

He took a few steps and looked over his shoulder, scowling when she didn't immediately follow. "Well?"

"I thought you wanted to work."

"Don't put words in my mouth. I said I wanted to go to my office." His eyes grew slumberous, red heat sparking. "I didn't say I wanted to work."

8

Hades was in a strange mood. He could trace his off-kilter emotions to the moment Persephone had given him that tiny bit of her power. He didn't know if it was the power or her actions or her words afterwards that made him feel almost...happy.

He'd understated the matter—deities were virulently opposed to sharing their powers. Hell, he didn't know if he'd ever give anyone even a smidgen of his hoarded strength. But she did it easily, simply so he could defeat a worthless demon wielding a tiny toothpick of a spear. When she'd discovered exactly what happened, she wasn't even horrified, but accepted it calmly. And then she went and complimented him, acted like she understood where he was coming from. And then *saved* him, looked all cute and delighted to finally have some smidgen of control over her power.

You're remarkable.

Remarkable! What did that even mean.

It was enough to make him confused. Confused and horny.

Persephone preceded him into his office. He shut the door loudly. The click of the lock made her jump. He liked it when she was a little unsure. The hint of vulnerability appealed to him, particularly when she was doing her lady-of-the-manor act the rest of the time.

Keeping her guessing was a fun game, so instead of rushing to get her naked, he went to his desk and sat in his chair. He took his time making himself comfortable before crooking his finger at her in a way that he was certain would raise her blood pressure.

She didn't love orders, his Persephone. Indeed, her eyes narrowed, and he waited for her to snort at his imperious, silent command.

But a small smile curved her lips, and she sashayed over to stand in front of him, her dress rippling and briefly defining her legs.

He raised a brow. "You're in the mood to obey me?"

"I suppose so."

"Why?"

Her smile grew wider. "Because you want me to disobey you."

Fuck, but she could read him like a book, and he didn't like that. He was so contrary, he wanted to reward her earlier kind words and actions by proving her wrong, proving that he was no saint. His dominant, autocratic side stretched out of slumber, not that it ever rested for long. "Take off your dress. With your hands," he added, so she wouldn't simply dematerialize it.

She raised her hands to the buttons that ran along the front of the dress. Pearl buttons on a pale pink dress—it was his fantasy, his secret kink, innocence on the verge of being despoiled.

The little V of skin at her throat widened as she released

Hot as Hades

each button, showing him that glorious unblemished flesh. Every time he saw that skin, his selfish, territorial nature made him want to mark it, to claim it as his. He had to forcibly remind himself that Persephone and her skin's presence in his life was strictly temporary.

A snarl sounded, and he realized by her startled expression that it came from him. She would leave him sooner or later.

But for now...for now, she was his. *Focus on this moment.*

And there was so much to focus on, particularly when she shrugged the dress off her shoulders, surprising him with the lacy white corset she wore underneath. The garment propped up her breasts, her nipples peeking out from the lace like confections on a cupcake. It was sensory overload, the erotic snatches of her body almost too much to take in at once. Corset. No panties. Garters. A combination of silken flesh and material.

He realized he had been staring at her without speaking when she shifted her weight. "Touch yourself," he ordered.

A flush spread over her exposed breasts. "Where?"

Anywhere. Everywhere. "Your tits. Play with them." He deliberately used the cruder word, wanting to shock her into refusing him, perverse bastard that he was.

She didn't refuse him, though, simply cupped those gloriously full mounds. Her fingers worked the hard nipples, her head falling back with a small moan as she massaged them.

His cock grew harder, pressing against the weight of his trousers, but he knew if he allowed himself release, it would be over before it began. Her legs spread wider as she toyed with her breasts. One delicate hand started to trail down her body to the open lips of her pussy.

Hades allowed her to get as far as her lower belly before

he spoke. "Stop." She didn't listen, her fingers tangling in her pubic hair.

"Persephone. Stop."

She jerked and stared at him, confused and primed for release.

"Come here." Hades swore the heady scent of sun and flowers clung to her skin, wafting under his nose as she walked closer to him. "Turn around."

She hesitated but turned when he made a twirling gesture. Her ass was full and round, bare but framed by the garter and corset. It made an enticing picture.

Paying no attention to her jump of surprise, he palmed a cheek and roughly massaged the flesh. "I love your ass," he murmured. "I love your whole body. It's like it was made for me. Only for me."

It took him a second to realize the import of what he'd bleated aloud. Growling in frustration at himself, he grabbed her hips and spun her around. She teetered, steadying after she grasped his forearms for balance.

"Take me out," he demanded. He spread his legs to give her room to work the buttons on his trousers, which were stretched tight over the bulge of his erection. The slightly bent-over position she was in made her tits hang down like ripe fruit. Unable to resist, he leaned forward and licked the top of those mounds, finding them delicious as usual. She stiffened, her hands stopping their work. He released his hold on the chair's arms to cradle her breasts and bring them to his mouth. He knew what pleased her. She always liked it when he sucked hard, lashing at the nipple with his tongue, so he did that now, bringing a high-pitched cry from her mouth.

"Don't stop," he drew away to tell her. "Take me out. Play with me."

Hot as Hades

She trembled. He loved it when he made her shake with need. It made him feel ten feet tall. "I can't concentrate," she said.

He released her, giving no heed to her pitiful whimper. "Then I'll stop distracting you."

"Jerk."

The word lacked heat, and he grinned. He'd come to read her body well, and he knew she needed him badly. "On your knees, goddess. Maybe that will help you focus."

She shot him a mock-glare. Her fingers resumed their mission as she sank to the subservient position.

He had to grit his teeth as those delicate fingers touched and rubbed him through the leather. When she finally managed to get the fly open, his cock almost ran out to greet her, pushing into her hands. The blessed feel of her warm palm over him made him want to shout for joy and pump into her hand for as long as necessary to get him off.

"Persephone..." He shoved his hips up, groaning as her hand slipped up the shaft and back down, the better to feel that softness all around him.

"What order would you like to give me now, Lord Hades?"

He slit his eyes at her mocking emphasis on *Lord*. Impertinent baggage. "Make me come."

Her hand jacked him again, and he spread his legs wider, an invitation to continue. Idly, as if she wasn't kneeling at his feet in a scandalous corset and playing with his naked cock, she tilted her head. "With my hands? Or my mouth?"

He swallowed, the thought of Persephone's lips wrapped around his cock filling his head. He had a particular fondness for blowjobs but had rarely been able to find anyone who was willing to bestow that favor. Because he was bigger and more powerful than most, he always had the distasteful impression that he was forcing his partner.

However, if Persephone chose to grace him with her mouth... He said nothing, and she smiled. "I do remember you saying something about drinking your come." His cock jerked at the memory, the dirty words he'd roughly muttered while lost in a haze of sexual need. Without any warning, she licked the vein running along the side of his cock. He gasped, and his hands flew to her shoulders, the little lick punching into his stomach.

"I guess you like this," he half-heard her say. Unable to care if her tone held the proper amount of respect for him, he threaded his hands through her hair.

"More," he said, aware that he was pleading.

Her mouth surrounded him, her tongue and the insides of her cheeks warm and silken wet. He had the fleeting thought that this was as foreign to her as it was to him, as she was delightfully awkward in figuring out how to move her lips and tongue and hands in tandem with each other. She learned quickly though, and within a few minutes she was officially driving him out of his mind.

PERSEPHONE DECIDED blowjobs weren't exactly a bad thing. In fact, sucking Hades's cock could very well be her favorite thing. It filled her with an immense sense of power, to have this huge god at her mercy. And he was definitely at her mercy. His body was rigid in the seat, his hands filled with her hair. She didn't feel trapped or forced, but entwined, the contact of his fingers in the strands bonding him to her.

Mentally, she snorted. Such poetic imagery for a blatantly crude act.

Hot as Hades

She pushed thoughts of poetry out of her head as she closed her eyes and sucked him deeper, loving his cock in her mouth. It felt even bigger to her this way, with her eyes closed and unable to see the matching proportion of the rest of his body.

"Deeper," he rasped, and she obeyed, suddenly wanting this to be the best, most mind-blowing sexual experience of his long life, wanting him ruined for other women, wanting him to remember her forev—

Nope, not going there.

His hands became more insistent as he gripped her hair, but she welcomed the tiny tug of pain. It centered her, made her focus even more on the responses of his body.

"Sephie," he moaned. She mentally smiled. She'd never tell him, but she liked the never-before-used diminutive of her name. It made her feel cherished. "Harder." His hips bucked up, his shaft almost choking her. With a soft noise, he stroked her hair when she would have gagged. "Hush. You can take it." He dragged his hips down, and then gave another more cautious thrust. The tip of his cock breached her throat. She held it there, prepared for it this time, and breathed through her nose. She was awarded with his harsh grunt as he withdrew and did it again.

As sexy as his powerful movements were, she wanted the chance to play too, and if she continued deep-throating him, he would come quickly. Though he was caught in the grip of a lustful haze, he stilled as soon as she rested her hands on his thighs and exerted pressure.

She rewarded him by bobbing her head up and down, taking more of his shaft each time, dying to absorb all of him. He made a rough noise and relaxed back into the chair, giving her implicit permission to learn his body.

He liked it when she lashed him with her tongue. When

she scraped her teeth along the side of him, he bowed in his chair.

And when she sucked his balls, he swore loudly, gripped her hair harder and directed her back to his cock.

Wild with her own arousal, she released him and dragged her hand down her body, fingering her soaking-wet pussy. He hadn't even touched her yet, not really, and her body was practically dripping in need.

"Are you wet?"

Her mouth full of cock, she nodded, glancing up at him.

A smile curved his hard lips. "Poor girl, when you're doing such a good job of sucking my cock. Here, let me help you. Remove your hand, and get up on your knees. Spread your legs."

Hesitant, not quite sure what he was about, she took her hand away and did as he said. And promptly gasped at what felt like Hades's cock entering her pussy. Hades's cock, which was firmly captured in her mouth. Her gaze flew to his, and his nostrils flared, those black-and-red eyes burning. "Do you like that?"

There was no energy to respond.

"Nod or I'll take it away." The phantom cock gave a few tentative thrusts.

She nodded, fearful that this extraordinary sensation would disappear.

"I like to watch your eyes when I sink into you. They go all big and dark, like you can't believe you're getting fucked by me. It makes me even harder, longer." He was harder in her mouth, heat rising from his body as the cock inside her pussy began thrusting in earnest. "I like this too. It's even hotter when your mouth is stuffed full of cock at the same time as your pussy. Since I wouldn't let another man near you, this is the only way I can see you like this, but I'm okay with that. Do you want to be fucked harder?"

She nodded and then moaned as the cock inside her pussy started pounding into her. The thrusts were so vigorous it pushed her even harder against the cock in her mouth. Cupping her head, he began fucking her face in earnest, and she allowed him, overwhelmed by the power within this lustful god, and more, of the strength he kept checked to keep from hurting her.

He worked in tandem so she was never quite empty, one cock filling her as the other withdrew, until Hades's thrusts in her mouth turned erratic and wild, and he lost the concentration necessary to keep up the illusory dick filling her pussy. She tightened her vaginal muscles around the suddenly aching emptiness, and tightened her mouth around him, needing to climax almost as badly as she wanted this huge male to come in her mouth.

"Finish me," he gasped, and she fondled his balls, rolling them in her hand. He stiffened and shoved his cock deep inside of her, groaning as he ejaculated. She swallowed everything he gave her. When he finished, she attempted to pull away, but his fingers were tangled in her hair. He worked his hand free from the snarls. She glanced up at him when she was finally released, and he stared at her, her slumberous, decadent Lord, replete and utterly relaxed. "Clean me up, goddess."

She could have protested the arrogant command, but she obeyed for the selfish reason that it was another opportunity to tease him, to taste him. His penis was only semihard now, but it wouldn't take him long to recover—particularly if she helped him along.

HADES LOOKED down at the glorious goddess who had taken him to heaven and back, and he wondered fleetingly if he'd ever had any better. She literally cleaned him up, licking his cock and balls and stomach as if she was starving for the taste of his come, as if she hadn't already drunk him dry.

Well, not completely dry, he realized as he quickly became hard again under her ministrations. She enveloped him, sucked him all the way down to his root. When she withdrew, his cock stood at attention, red and aroused and covered in her saliva. She trailed a finger down it and stood, gesturing for him to move his chair back.

Intrigued, he complied. He had to restrain a whimper when she turned gracefully and leaned over his desk. Her eyes speared him as she cast him a glance over her shoulder, filled with lust and desire. "My turn. I want it like this."

Thank the gods she'd sucked him off, because the position, with her ass framed by those white garters, and the corset, would have made him come in his pants like a randy youth.

"It is your turn," he purred, and watched the shiver race down her spine. His lady was ridiculously easy to arouse. He only had to speak in a certain tone, and he could smell her getting wetter. He loved it.

He stood as she bowed her head, her body prepared for him to ram into what he was sure was her soaking-wet cunt. Still, he couldn't resist stroking her buttocks, the flesh so nicely offered up for him.

"What are you waiting for?"

He lightly tapped her ass cheek, loving how it gave way to the small smack. "Hush."

"Fuck me."

"I need to make sure you're ready." He moved his hands to her hips, tightening his fingers enough for her to realize she was trapped, and pulled her back a step, pushing her body lower onto the desk in an exaggerated arch.

"Trust me, I'm ready." Her tone was plaintive and desperate.

He slipped his hand into her pretty muff and made an appreciative noise. "You are ready. I don't think I've ever felt you so wet."

Her body shook in silent laughter. "You bastard. Hurry up. I'm dying."

"As my lady commands. I am nothing if not agreeable." He pressed his cock into her sweet pussy, savoring the tight and slick heaven, as well as her gasp. He leaned over her so his front was plastered against her back and breathed into her ear. "Did you like getting double fucked?"

"You know I did."

He shoved himself deep and then materialized the sensation of something probing at her tight little anus. "We'll go for a triple next time."

She was so still below him as he pumped in and out of both of her holes, he wondered if she was breathing, until she gave a mighty shudder. "Yes...anything you want."

The words were a dangerous thing to say to a god. His mind ran wild with all of the things he could demand of Persephone. Her body. Her soul.

Her heart.

He pulled her up so he could access the front of her body, giving special attention to her breasts and the hard little clit at the top of her sex. Her hips worked back against him and he let her use him, keeping the rhythm of his thrusts hard and deep until she fell apart in his arms, her loud moans punctuating each squeeze of his cock.

When he knew she was satiated, he withdrew. His penis

felt wet and cold and extremely unhappy to be out of her, so he rolled her onto her back and penetrated her again.

Since both of them had taken the edge off, that usual frenzied need wasn't present. Hades moved in her languidly, the sounds of their bodies and panting breath the only noise in the otherwise silent room. As he thrust inside of her, he stroked her sides, her breasts, finally wrapping his hands in hers, palm to palm, fingers entwined.

He leaned down and kissed her. Their kisses were always desperate, but this was calm and serene, a leisurely duel of tongues, a gentle sipping at her lips. He only sped up the pace of his hips because he felt the mood was becoming too mushy. "I'm never going to be able to look at my desk the same again."

She laughed, but there was something sad in her eyes. So he kissed her again, tasting the passion and desire in her mouth while at the same time making it impossible to see what she was thinking and feeling.

When he came, he buried his face in her neck and inhaled deeply, knowing that his words hadn't been a lie. His productivity was forever shot—he'd never be able to see anything but Persephone in this room, naked and giving and warm.

9

A leafy branch smacked Hades on the side of his head, disturbing him from the ledgers he was going over. "What the—?" He glanced at the smaller armchair next to his large one and smiled at the vines securely entwined in Persephone's hair. Her nose was firmly poked in a book. "Sephie. You're growing green again."

"What—? Oh for crying out loud." She sighed and jerked away from the vines. He winced for her at what he was sure was a healthy yank on her hair. The drooping vegetation made a halfhearted motion back toward her, but when she raised a finger, the vine instead turned around and slithered along the arm of her chair...perilously close to his.

"Don't even think about it," he muttered to the thing, wishing he hadn't promised Persephone he wouldn't make the plants go kaboom. Luckily, it responded to the menace in his voice and wilted. "What are you so absorbed in, anyway?"

She closed the book. "An old treatise I found on how to open portals."

"I could teach you more than a book."

She shot him a glance that made him want to forget the fact that he'd already ravaged her three times that day. "You already have. I can never thank you enough."

He squirmed, uncomfortable with her gratitude. He might have helped her focus and taught her some parlor tricks, but the power was hers and hers alone. "Stop."

"Seriously. I don't feel weak anymore. If it wasn't for you—"

"I did nothing. But if you want to thank me, bring me some of those grapes from that table."

She picked up the bowl of grapes sitting on the table closest to her. He waited 'til she stood closer and then wrapped his arm around her, pulling her down to his lap. "I want you too. Feed me, woman." She held a plump grape to his mouth, and he bit down.

"How is it?"

"Not as tasty as you."

Her face softened. "You sweet talker, you."

When she talked to him in that low, intimate voice and sat in his arms, he felt sweet. He felt...like a good deity, and not one of evil.

She fed him another grape, squealing when he bit at her fingers. "I miss food."

He turned his head away from the next grape she started to feed him. "You didn't tell me that. I thought you didn't care, or I wouldn't have eaten in front of you."

"It's a comfort thing. Of course you should eat." She tapped the grape against his lips. "Open, sesame."

He kept his head averted. "No. I don't need it."

"But you like it. Please, I don't want to be the reason you go without."

"Then how do I feel, knowing I'm the reason you go without?"

They were silent for a minute, both of them cognizant of the fact that they'd been tiptoeing around their emerging feelings for the past months they'd been together, neither quite willing to be the first to declare themselves. "Persephone..."

She kissed him, warm, openmouthed, and as always, he responded, unable to do anything but. When she pulled away, she slipped the grape between his lips. He shook his head as he bit down. "Sneaky."

"Mmm." She wiped her thumb across the trace of juice on his lip and stared at it. He pulled it to his mouth and licked it off, lest she be tempted to taste it herself.

Why stop her? Fool.

More and more, he called himself that, wondering if he should simply resort to trickery or magic to keep her with him always. It would be easy to fool her into eating or drinking something. Or after he received the all clear to send her back, he could pretend his powers were still blocked. She would believe him. Then he could wrap her in magic, make it so no god, Zeus or otherwise, could extract her from his Underworld.

She snuggled closer, and he knew there was no chance of him resorting to any of those tactics. He couldn't bear it if her warm glances eventually filled with trapped hatred, if she came to believe that the stories and rumors and the role he played for others, a monster and debauched and hate-filled god, was true. Better to hold her for the time he had, and then let her go.

For some other god to take her?

"Your teeth are grinding, Hades. Are you okay?"

He deliberately unclenched his teeth and grinned down at her. "Fine. I—" He looked up at the empty room, suddenly alert. "Did you feel that?"

"Yes." Persephone jumped up and, to his surprise, stood in front of him, her stance battle ready. "What is that? It feels like a storm, or..."

"Lightning," he finished grimly, and stepped in front of her, stopping her when she tried to scurry to his side. "Stay."

"I'm not a pet."

"No, I wouldn't be quite so worried about a pet."

"What's going on?"

"Get ready. Zeus is about to break a treaty as old as time and piss me off all at the same time." He had beefed up his barriers since Persephone had arrived, but apparently not enough.

A little hand patted him on his shoulder, as if he were a horse in need of gentling. "Don't go losing your temper, now. Let's talk to him first."

"I suppose I should serve him tea too—"

A flash of bright light cut him off, and his brother was standing before him, looking fit and respectable in a three-piece suit. "Brother!" Zeus cried, and opened his arms wide, like he actually expected a fucking hug.

"You have one minute," Hades said softly, "to explain why the fuck you're down here, and it better be a good-ass reason to intrude in my world."

Zeus had the temerity to look hurt. "I can't believe you don't show me any hospitality, big brother." He glanced around, his eyes widening. "Is this your study? It's a little dark, isn't it? But then, you always were partial to dark colors."

No, actually, he had loved yellows and greens and blues. The unbidden thought popped into his head, a reminder of the times as a young god that he had reveled in wandering in the clouds. It was only after a few centuries down here that he had come to appreciate the darker shades. "You think I'm joking? I've only just forgiven you for piercing my world to send Persephone and interfering with my powers. Now you dare to break our vow to one another and barge into my world in person?"

With each word his voice rose. Persephone started patting him on the back. The attempt to soothe him was in vain.

Zeus's face chilled, his eyes growing arctic cold. "Watch how you speak to me, Hades."

"Fuck you."

"I can level this whole world with little more than a thought, you know."

Aaaand, this was why they kept to their own worlds. His temper spiked to molten-lava levels. The floor trembled, and in the distance, lightening crashed. "You so much as breathe on my domain, I will use your clouds for fucking target practice."

"Whoa, whoa." Persephone ducked out from under his arm and stood in front of him, one hand resting securely on his chest. "Let's all calm down here, shall we? Why don't we see what Zeus wants first?"

"Persephone." Insult forgotten, smile wide, Zeus moved to hug her, brows rising when Hades growled and jerked her back against his chest. "Ah. That's how it is, is it? No worries, Hades, I have no lustful intentions toward our little peony."

"Bullshit. You have lustful intentions toward everyone."

"Well, not everyone." Zeus considered that. "There was this crone..."

"Why. Are. You. Here?" Hades asked at the same time Persephone said, "Zeus, what do you want?"

"Oh. Yes. Demeter sent me."

An unwelcome jolt. His arms tightened around Persephone. "What?"

Zeus examined his buffed fingernails. "She's despondent over Persephone being gone. She's telling everyone that Hades here abducted her."

"What?" Persephone shook her head. "Why didn't you tell her that you sent me here for protection?"

"I did." Zeus scowled. "I think."

Hades really didn't care what anyone thought about his reputation, but his heart warmed when Persephone stiffened. "What do you mean, you think? His character's being assassinated for no reason."

"Sweetheart, Hades doesn't really *have* a character. Anyway, she's so unhappy, she's completely neglected the harvest."

"But the humans will starve."

"Mmm. Lots of them already have."

"But I haven't been here for long at all."

"Time moves slower there, chickie. It's been, what, about nine months mortal time? Demeter's pretty much been roaming the world, wailing about her baby. She won't lift a finger to do any actual work."

"Oh no..." Persephone turned in Hades's arms. He tried to relax them, to let her go, but the dread in his belly only made him hold her tighter. "I have to go to her, Hades. I can't let all those people suffer."

"I'm so sorry, Persephone, but you can't go back," Zeus said, sounding almost bored.

"Surely the danger has passed."

"The danger? Oh, yeah, the other gods. Yeah, there's, uh, no threat anymore."

Hades narrowed his eyes.

"But you must have eaten or drunk something while you've been here. You probably didn't know this, but that means you must stay here...forever!" He raised his arms high with the last word and punctuated it with a thunderclap.

They both stared at him. "I didn't eat anything. I knew what the consequences of that would be."

Zeus lowered his hands, his brow crinkling. "You did?"

She nodded.

He looked at Hades, confusion in his gaze. "And you didn't try to trick her?"

Hades shook his head slowly. No. But oh, how he wished he had.

Persephone rubbed his jaw, and he wanted to close his eyes to savor these moments, what he knew were the last touches he'd ever feel from her. "I have to go, Hades. I can't stay here while innocents suffer," she whispered.

No, she couldn't, and he wouldn't expect her to. If he spoke, his voice would crack, and he couldn't afford to show weakness in front of his power-hungry brother, so he dipped his head in acknowledgement.

Her eyes were wet as they searched his, and he had to glance away for fear he would also break down. He allowed her to lead his head down and press a brief, chaste kiss against his lips. Her fingers followed the path of her lips and brushed his mouth. She turned in a flurry and addressed Zeus as she walked quickly to the door. "I need to pack a few things. Please wait for me here."

Hades watched her go, knowing that he would replay the sight of her leaving him in his mind for centuries to come.

The silence was absolute after he left, until Zeus let out a long sigh. "You fucked that up, brother."

There was no energy left to snarl at the other god. Hades walked to his armchair and sank down into it, feeling old and tired.

Zeus sat in Persephone's chair—how had she made it her own in such a short time?—and materialized a bottle of ambrosia and a goblet. "You look like you need this."

"Yes." Hades rolled his head against the back of the chair and accepted the wine. "There never was a troupe of horny gods, was there?"

"Nope."

"Why?"

Zeus didn't pretend to misunderstand. "Because the Fates saw it, and it was taking you two too damn long to get together."

"The Fates saw..."

"You and Persephone. Your lives..." He wound his fingers together. "They're intertwined."

"Usually you don't give a fuck what the Fates say."

"I do when they tell me it was...what was it? Vitally critical for the cosmic balance that you two come together."

"Vitally critical?"

"Yeah. Heavy stuff. They finally begged me to do something."

"No one begs you to do anything. You're selfish to the bone, Zeus."

A flush covered the god's face. "To be honest, I wouldn't be averse to having Persephone as far from Olympus as possible for my own reasons. She's a sweet child, but that power..."

A flash of pride went through Hades, that it was his

Persephone inspiring that note of jealous reverence. Before he remembered that she wasn't his, of course. He studied the amber liquid in the goblet he held. "She doesn't know who her parents are. Do you?" Once, the question had been important, but now it was simply a way to think of something other than her impending departure.

As cagey as Zeus was, he was also an incurable office gossip. "I suppose since you two are *finis*, I can tell you. She has no parents."

"Parthenogenesis." The asexual form of reproduction wasn't completely uncommon.

"Kind of. She was created from a shard of Gaia's power."

Somehow, he wasn't surprised. Gaia was the Earth. It fit. "I see."

"Demeter also contains a lesser shard, which is why the two of them draw strength from one another."

"Why haven't you told her?"

"We don't want her to get all full of herself, now do we?"

No, you don't want her to know her own strength. Bastard.

"Don't say anything to her."

"Of course not," he lied. He'd find some way to let her know the truth. "I knew there was a more selfish reason for you sending her down here. Good deeds, even for cosmic balance purposes, are not your usual schtick."

Zeus couldn't even try to look offended. "You know how our kind is."

"What about the whole, *don't think about keeping her with you, the Earth needs her* line?"

"It wasn't a line. As you can see, the Earth does need her. However, more pertinent to me, doing this put the Fates at my mercy. So I figured, I'll drop Persephone down here, keep you from sending her back for a while, bada-bing, you'll somehow trick her into staying forever, so when Demeter does her expected tantrum, I can say, so sorry, Persephone's stuck." Zeus shook his head. "I didn't count on your overdeveloped conscience. I have no idea what this means." He frowned. "Maybe this time was all that the Fates meant for you to have."

It wasn't enough. That was cruel. Yet the Fates never pretended to be kind. He tried to concentrate on the rest of Zeus's words. "I don't have an overdeveloped conscience."

"Sure you do. Way more than me."

"That's because you have no conscience."

"I do too. For instance, it's always bothered me that I cheated."

"What?"

Zeus leaned back and propped his ankle on his knee, utterly relaxed. "All those eons ago. I cheated. When we drew lots for who got what kingdom, I fixed it so you would get the Underworld."

Hades stared at his brother. Ordinarily, he would have blown up at this revelation of trickery and all of its implications, but his heart was too heavy. Zeus had always known the best times to deliver bad news.

"Why would you do that?"

"Because it was the most important."

"What?"

"Look, there's my place, the sky, but I'm a pretty hands-off kind of guy. The mortals on Earth are all there for such a short time, so I don't have to really do anything but keep the others up in the clouds happy and in line. I knew I'd do well in the sky. I knew Poseidon wouldn't be able to handle anything more demanding than fish or maybe a mermaid, so I made sure he got the water."

Hades opened his mouth, but then closed it again. The

last time Poseidon had talked to him, he'd kept calling him *bruh*. He was well suited for the easy, aqueous lifestyle.

"But then there was the Underworld. This is where the mortal's eternal soul goes, brother. It required someone who was just and decent and hardworking. You were the only one of us who showed a glimmer of any potential. So I made sure you got it."

"Don't flatter me."

"I'm not, damn it. Do you think I like feeling like I'm lacking in something? Seriously?" Zeus looked sober for the first time that Hades could ever recall. "I'm sorry things didn't work out with you and Persephone. I guess I had hoped that over the years you'd gotten so desperate... Well, never mind. I figure you'll be firming up your world now so I won't be able to pierce it again."

"Yes." Now that Zeus had come through physically, it would be easier to see where the weakness in his defenses existed. Though right now, he wanted to rip down all the barriers so anyone could come in, so Persephone would find her way back. That previous territoriality was gone, as if it had never existed.

But he wasn't the only one who resided here, and he had a whole kingdom of souls to protect and keep safe. So the barrier would stay up, bigger and badder than before, particularly from his meddling little brother.

As if he was reading his thoughts, Zeus sighed. "Very well. If you'll excuse me, I'll go get Persephone."

Hades couldn't speak as Zeus left, his heart too heavy to allow anything as mundane as words to leave it.

PERSEPHONE COULDN'T SEEM to stop crying, though she knew that there was little her tears could actually accomplish.

She'd materialized a suitcase, but all she had wanted to put in it so far was the black rose Hades had given her from Tartarus, still as fresh and velvety as the day he'd conjured it. She cradled it to her cheek. How could she leave him?

Sure, there were things she didn't love about the Underworld itself. She missed her meadow, and sunshine, and fresh air. But it wasn't all bad here…because here had Hades.

She allowed the rose to soak in her tears and finally, with a sigh, got to her feet. She ignored the suitcase and her open closet—she could materialize any garment she wished now, thanks to Hades. She drifted to her dresser and placed the rose on it, prepared to leave it behind as well.

"Don't cry."

She sniffed and turned to find Zeus in the doorway. Lines of distress marred his otherwise boyishly handsome face. She'd always liked this god, particularly when he'd allowed the rumor to spread that she was his daughter, giving her some extra protection when she'd been a powerless goddess. She didn't need that protection now. "Is it time, then?"

"It is." Zeus hesitated. "I need to get something off my chest. Especially since you'll learn the truth as soon as we get back."

Intrigued, she motioned for him to continue.

"There never was any horde of horny gods after you. Well, of course, there are always amorous gods, many of whom would love to get their hands on you, but there was never any plot, per se. So there's no need for you to be scared to return."

A pounding started in her skull. "Wait…so why did you send me here?"

As he told her, her anger mounted steadily, until her vision was covered in a red haze. "So let me get this straight," she said with admirable calm. "You played with two people's lives because you wished to curry the favor of the Fates?"

"That makes it sound cheap. Hey, where did that ivy come from?"

Her previous liking for the god vanished, and her temper snapped. A nervous shout ripped from his chest when a thick vine burst up from the ground and wrapped around him from knee to neck. "Now, Persephone, I like being tied up as much as the next guy, but..." She let him struggle a little bit, and she knew he was trying to break the hold of the greens. She was as surprised as he was when he stopped, obviously unable to. A dark emotion tightened his face. "You don't know what you're playing with, child."

Fire. Or lightning, to be more exact. "You don't know what *you're* playing with, Zeus. You think you can jerk me around? That I'll lie down and allow you to drag me from world to world?"

"If you had eaten something here, I wouldn't be able to drag you anywhere, damn it. And it's not like it's even too late now. Grab a bite, and I can leave you here."

"You know very well that if I stay here, Demeter will make innocent people suffer. I'd never be able to stand for that."

He jutted out his lip. "Well, I can't help you. As soon as I see you out, Hades will make the security so tight around this place, I'll never be able to ferry you back and forth. And no other god would have the power to do as I've done. Especially not a noob like you." He said it simply, with no conceit.

She tilted her head and considered his words. "This

noob has you immobilized, Zeus. I think I can manage quite a bit." She swept back to the dresser and grabbed the black rose. As she left the room in a jog, she made sure that the ivy would release the god shortly, long enough for her to have some alone time with Hades.

After all, she didn't want to totally piss Zeus off.

10

---

ades wasn't in his sitting room where she'd left him, and she was out of breath by the time she tracked him down to his formal receiving room, where he was conferring with Cerberus. Their conversation terminated when she came in. The pain in his gaze made her want to howl in agony. Every ounce of his sadness multiplied her own.

He dismissed Cerberus with a wave, and the dog paused as it passed her and formally bowed all three heads. Middle spoke. "I'm sorry to hear you are leaving, my lady. We will greatly miss you."

"Don't go, Persephone," Bob wailed.

She smiled through her torment and patted the dear pup's heads, even the silent killer on the right who leaned into her touch. "Please don't worry, Cerberus, this isn't goodbye. I'll be back," she said, loud enough for Hades to hear.

He lifted his head, a frown knitting his brow.

Cerberus bowed again and left, and Persephone wasn't sure whether it believed her or not. The door closed on Bob's disconsolate sobs. She crossed over to Hades slowly, some of her confidence falling away as she studied his face. It was wiped clean of emotion now, so impassive she might have imagined his previous heartache. "You haven't left yet."

"You knew that. You would feel it when I did."

He glanced down at his hands. "Yes, I would feel it."

"I don't have a lot of time, because Zeus is probably really mad I trapped him in a vine."

"You...what? Why?"

"Why isn't important. He made me angry so I...you know. Immobilized him."

"And it worked? He couldn't get free?"

She tried not to preen under the obvious admiration in his tone and face. "Ahem. Yes. Anyway. He'll be free soon, and then he'll take me away. You know that none of us have any choice about me going back."

She didn't mean for it to be a question, but he nodded anyway. "Yes. The mortals need you."

A deep inhale. "Let me come here again, Hades."

Poker face gone now, clear misery was written all over him. "I can't leave the world vulnerable to breaches, Sephie. Only those who belong here are supposed to come. Traveling back and forth is against the rules."

"Except for you." She clenched her hand around the black rose, turning her palm up and opening it again to display two black orchid blooms. Edible orchids. "Let me belong here."

He ignored her offering and continued to stare into her eyes. "You would be stuck here forever if you eat those."

"This is your world. Your power. You once told me I should make my power my bitch, manipulate it as I see fit, that I was the only one who should place limits on it." She extended her hand to him. "Give me some of your power, the ability to come

Hot as Hades

back and forth. Give me the option of seeing you again. I know how territorial you are about this world. Give me your trust and believe me when I say I won't abuse it."

He searched her face. "You could destroy my world."

"I could." Not a promising reaction, but she continued to hold out her hand. "You could destroy the mortal world, which needs me, by tricking me into staying with you for all time."

He swallowed, this big, strong god suddenly nervous and unsure. "I wouldn't ever do that."

"I know. And I won't hurt you. Or your world."

As if in slow motion, she watched his palm come down over hers, sealing the flowers between them.

The slight tremble in his fingers touched her heart. He waited a minute and then took his hand away. "It's done."

She looked down at the dark black-red pomegranate seeds that now lay in her hands. "That's it?"

"Yes."

The trust went both ways, she realized. He could very well have done nothing, and this could be trickery. No god would fault her for refusing to eat the seeds.

But she would fault herself. She quickly ate both of them as he watched her, eyes hooded. Nothing happened. "I don't feel any different." No, wait, was that a small burst of warmth in her belly? She pressed her hand against it.

"You may not. But you now have an all-access pass to the Underworld, Sephie. If you should wish to come back, ever, simply think of where you'd like to be, and your power should do the rest."

She didn't miss the qualifying *if*. "I will be back, Hades. Six mortal months to this day, at midnight, I'll be standing here again." Six months should give her time to figure out some way to calm Demeter and make provisions for the mortals who needed her.

"I'm so glad you're having fun planning your next rendezvous, however you plan on accomplishing that," Zeus spat as he stalked into the room. "I definitely won't be helping."

"I don't need your help." She stretched up on her tiptoes and kissed Hades on his mouth. "Be good. Don't flay too many souls while I'm gone."

"They always deserve it."

"I know."

Hades grasped her hand. "Six months, Sephie."

"Six months."

"By the way, you were created from a shard of Gaia's power."

She froze. Gaia? The Earth? She was created from the freakin' Earth? "What?"

"You son of a bitch. You promised," Zeus squawked.

"I lied," Hades replied easily. "They didn't want you to know because they worried you would become too strong."

"Gaia..." she said, touched by reverent awe. "Truly?"

"Truly."

"That's amazing."

He squeezed her hand. "You're amazing."

"If we're done here, can you move your ass, Persephone? I'm so fucking ready to get out of this place," Zeus griped.

Hades tugged her closer, trapping her against his chest in a hard hug. "Zeus." There was a trace of deadly menace in the one word.

Zeus did not appear to notice it. "What?"

"You talk to my lady in that tone again, I'll rip into your cloud and shove your lightning bolt up your ass. Do you understand?"

Persephone bit her lip to keep from laughing, particularly when Zeus cleared his throat and muttered a very indistinct, "Fine."

"And you will make sure the other gods comprehend that she's not to be toyed with, right?"

"Yes, yes. Come on...Lady Persephone."

Reluctantly, she let Hades go and walked over to Zeus. The other god slid his arm around her waist, and she could feel that little tug that would pull her out of this world and back to her own. Unable to resist, she turned around to catch a last glimpse of Hades's face.

Six months, she mouthed.

He nodded, but she knew him well enough to see the despondence in his face. *Six months*, she repeated silently to herself. There was no one on Heaven or Earth who could keep her away.

11

Six months.

Granted, six mortal months, so of course they'd flown by faster here, but still, each day had been brutal and grinding. His subjects had seen more of him than ever before. There were more than a few ghouls down in Tartarus who had heard of Persephone and were praying she would return almost as badly as he was.

Unable to take the stress, he growled and ripped at the choking noose wrapped around his neck. "What the hell is this tool of evil?"

"I believe it is called a tie, sire." Cerberus's middle head answered him as it critically studied the vase of flowers on a table. "Master, please sit."

Since sitting was no worse than standing, he dropped into his throne, propping his chin in his hand. "She won't recognize me wearing a shirt."

"Lady Persephone will be quite pleased."

"Do you think she'll play ball with me?" Bob wanted to know. Hades didn't answer, because it was hushed into silence by Middle.

Hot as Hades 103

He glanced at the new gold watch he wore, yet another trapping of civility he'd donned for Persephone. A minute. There was only a minute left until midnight.

"I'll leave you now, sire. Unless there's anything else you require?"

"No. Wait, Cerberus."

His servant turned. Hades swallowed. "If she doesn't come...make sure I'm okay in a few hours, all right? Make sure I'm here. Keep me here." Because if Cerberus didn't come, Hades knew the only viable choice would be to drink himself into a stupor. And if he went that route, the next step could involve something outlandish, like chasing after Persephone.

Middle nodded. "Very well, Lord Hades."

Cerberus took its leave, and Hades was alone with his thoughts and with the silent tick of his watch. Thirty seconds.

Twenty.

Ten.

He grasped the arms of his chair so hard, he was surprised they didn't turn to dust. Five.

Midnight.

He closed his eyes and opened them again, hoping something would be different, but the room was empty.

He waited another minute, counting the seconds again.

Nothing.

With a low groan, he cradled his head in his hands, unable to believe that she wasn't here. Unable to believe that he'd actually thought she would come back. Why the hell would she do that? Why would she care at all about coming back to an angry, foul-mouthed God who lived in an old dark palace with no windows, when she could go frolicking in a meadow whenever she felt like it? Hell, he could almost smell the scent of the flowers...

He stiffened at the same moment he heard her soft voice. "Hades?"

Raising his head, hardly daring to believe it, he found her standing there, as beautiful—no, more beautiful than—the day she left. Her hair was pulled back from her face, held by a thin circlet of gold flowers, the curls tumbling down her back. Her long gown was his favorite color, a dark red, cut low to show off her ample cleavage and cinched tight, reminding him of all the times he'd grasped that waist in his hands.

She raised her chin, and for the first time ever, he saw a split-second flash of the future instead of the past: a regal and intimidating Persephone ruling by his side. As he stood, she ruined her dignified mien by letting out a loud squeal and running straight toward him. He grabbed her up, glorying in the feel of her in his arms.

"You came back," he said, and he realized that he couldn't stop saying it. *You came back, you came back.*

"Oh, silly." She wrapped her legs around him and cupped his face in her hands. "You knew I'd come back."

"You're late." He kissed her desperately, thrilled when she responded. He had known, but there'd been a little sliver of doubt. When he allowed her air again, he whispered against the sweet-smelling curls at her temple. "You smell so good. You look so gorgeous."

"You aren't looking too shabby yourself. You look so handsome in a shirt."

He suddenly didn't regret Cerberus forcing him into the suit. "Don't leave me. Not again." Persephone leaned back, and he knew she wasn't going to be saying anything he liked.

Hot as Hades   105

"Actually..."

"No." With that autocratic edict, he tried to kiss her again, but she avoided his mouth. "Hades, listen to me."

"You're going to stay here. With me. No arguments. Now, sex."

Despite his extremely reasonable command, she unwrapped her legs from around him and squirmed out of his arms. "As great as that sounds, you need to listen to me. I had to make a deal to come down here."

He froze. "Who? Who did you make a deal with? I gave you the power to enter and leave at will, Sephie. You shouldn't have been making deals with anybody." Deals with gods and goddesses rarely ended well.

"Demeter."

He narrowed his eyes. "That..."

She covered his lips. "Hush. She loves me, and I love her, and whatever issues there may be between you, I won't let you badmouth her in my presence."

If the subject of this argument wasn't whiny Demeter, who was still somehow fucking with his life, he might actually be turned on as usual by no-nonsense Persephone. "What deal?" he said, his words muffled by her hand.

She removed her fingers from his lips and sighed. "We had a long talk. The shard Gaia gave her only really works in tandem with me. Without me there, Demeter can't ensure an adequate harvest for the mortals. I had no idea how much she, and the Earth, depended on my powers."

"They're important powers, Sephie."

Pride had her straightening her shoulders. "Yes, they are, aren't they? Even when I didn't really know how to use them, I was doing something right. And that means I have to go back at least once a year. I agreed that I would return to Demeter at the beginning of every harvest."

He tugged at the knot of the tie, suddenly hating it again. "For how long?"

"We talked about six months, and then nine..." She held up her hand when he growled. "Three. Just three mortal months. I do my thing, and I come back here."

"Three months is too long. Tell her a week."

She smiled. "Even I'm not powerful enough to get everything done in a week, Hades."

He loved the mantle of subtle confidence she wore now. "How long are you going to keep up this commute back and forth, Persephone?"

She sobered. "I guess...for however long you want me."

"Forever." There was no uncertainty in his soul, so there was no uncertainty in his voice.

Her throat worked. "Even knowing that I'll have to go back to Demeter every year? Because it's not only that I can't abandon the mortals. I need to soak up the sun and the elements of the Earth to sustain myself. Which makes sense, now that I know I'm a part of it."

"Yes. I don't like that, I'll be honest, but I'll figure out how to deal with it." Because she wouldn't be the goddess she was if she didn't agree to do this. In her shoes, he would do the same. So even though it went against his territorial nature, he'd work out his own issues and kiss her goodbye on her little trip home every year.

And he'd try to keep his cursing at Demeter in his head.

He nodded to the new smaller throne next to his. "The Underworld needs a queen, Persephone. And I need you. Will you rule by my side?"

Her eyes widened as she took in the addition to the room. "Really?"

"What did you think I meant when I said forever?" He puffed his chest. "I'm an honorable god. I wouldn't expect you to stay here and be my plaything." Or rather, not *only* his plaything.

"Oh, Hades. Of course I will."

"You'll have to put up with my temper and jealousy and possessiveness."

"You'll have to deal with my disappearances...well, really just that, I'm perfect otherwise. Ouch!" she yelped when he smacked her ass, but she was grinning. "Thank you for my throne. It's beautiful."

"I told them to carve flowers instead of skulls into it."

"That's so thoughtful, my darling."

"Can we have sex now?"

She blinked up at him, and just like that they were both naked. She pressed up against him. He growled as they kissed, pulling her back until he was seated in his throne and she was straddling him.

He muttered a curse as she slowly took him in. "I love you, you know."

Those slumberous emerald eyes beamed up at him. Somehow her lush body simultaneously held him captive and was at his mercy. "Of course. I love you too."

And as she took him to heaven, Hades knew that no matter how much she traveled in and out of his world, Persephone would never leave his heart.

ALSO BY ALISHA RAI

Modern Love

The Right Swipe

Girl Gone Viral

First Comes Like

Forbidden Hearts

Hate to Want You

Wrong to Need You

Hurts To Love You

Campbell Siblings Series

A Gentleman in the Street

Bedroom Games Series

Play With Me

Risk & Reward

Bet On Me

Pleasure Series

Glutton For Pleasure

Serving Pleasure

Fantasy Series

Be My Fantasy

Stay My Fantasy

The Karimi Siblings

Falling For Him

Waiting For Her

Single Title

Night Whispers

Hot as Hades

Never Have I Ever

Cabin Fever

ABOUT THE AUTHOR

Alisha Rai pens award-winning contemporary romances and her novels have been named Best Books of the Year by Washington Post, NPR, Amazon, Entertainment Weekly, Kirkus, Oprah Magazine, and Cosmopolitan Magazine. When she's not writing, Alisha is traveling or tweeting or tiktoking. To find out more about her books or to sign up for her newsletter, visit www.alisharai.com.

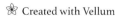

Copyright © 2010, 2021 by Alisha Rai

Cover: Designs By Priyanka

All rights reserved.

No part of this book may be reproduced in any form or by any electronic or mechanical means, including information storage and retrieval systems, without written permission from the author, except for the use of brief quotations in a book review.

❀ Created with Vellum

Printed in Great Britain
by Amazon